STRANGE HEART BEATING

Eli Goldstone

Strange Heart Beating

GRANTA

Granta Publications, 12 Addison Avenue, London W11 4QR

First published in Great Britain by Granta Books, 2017

A CIP catalogue record for this book is available from the British Library.

1 3 5 7 9 10 8 6 4 2

ISBN 978 1 78378 349 6
eISBN 978 1 78378 351 9

Typeset by Avon DataSet Limited, Bidford on Avon, B50 4JH

Printed and bound by CPI Group (UK) Ltd, Croydon, CR0 4YY

MIX
Paper from
responsible sources
FSC® C020471

for Kyle, of course

A sudden blow: the great wings beating still
Above the staggering girl, her thighs caressed
By the dark webs, her nape caught in his bill,
He holds her helpless breast upon his breast.

How can those terrified vague fingers push
The feathered glory from her loosening thighs?
And how can body, laid in that white rush,
But feel the strange heart beating where it lies?

W. B. Yeats

Here is the story of how the women in the Kauss family died. In 1825 Alma Kauss froze to death in the javelin of a pine tree's shadow, covered in grey-green needles. The man who patrolled the woods looking for this sort of thing (the dead) pointed out that the needles had fallen because the tree's provenance was not Latvia but Ukraine, and that it had lost its needles due to the strong winds that come in off the coast of the Baltic Sea. He had become aware over the past few years of the fact that trees of non-Latvian origin were being planted in Latvian soil.

'This is why,' he said, 'the tree will die.'

The tree did die, but not until many years later.

Her sister Marta died from choking on a pine cone while she was sleeping.

Neither of the younger Kauss sisters had children, but the eldest sister, Clara, their senior by four and a half years, had six children and lived until the age of ninety-nine. She died on her bed, urinating and choking, like most people.

Every death is an event but for the sake of my story let's say that this one wasn't, and continue.

The six sons of Clara Kauss died uneventfully.

The wife of the youngest son was also called Marta. She died when a chandelier fell in the home of the family for whom she had cleaned every day for twelve years. She was treated fairly and paid well. The chandelier fell only inches from crushing her crouching frame and she went home and told her husband and they prayed. Unbeknownst to Marta and her husband, she had picked up a shard in her heel. The wound grew badly infected under a layer of sloppily administered dressing and she died of sepsis, after a few days of confusion and anxiety and rapid breathing that her husband found alarming but also strangely alluring. They made love several times before she died, her chest slick with sweat and her eyes rolling back in her head.

She was pregnant.

Leda Kauss, my late wife, was the great-grandniece of Marta Kauss. She lived in North London, where she had acquired a laissez-faire attitude towards death through the telling and re-telling of these stories.

'There's this apocryphal tale,' she would say, while filling our visitor's glass with wine and smiling in a way that acknowledged the outrageousness of what she was about to say. 'My God!' they would reply. She never tired of talking about death, though whether she found it entertaining or just repeated herself out of some unconscious superstition (to ward off evil, I want to say, whatever that means), I can't know for sure.

She was an artist, a naturalist. She died in the boating lake of a local park, when one of the swans became alarmed at her proximity to its babies and attacked the boat, capsizing it and drowning Leda. It was a Wednesday afternoon and the weather was fine. Her hat floated up and bobbed on the subsiding currents like the yolk of an egg. I wasn't there to witness it but as soon as I was told the circumstances of her death I knew that that was the way it had been. The sun was round and yellow too. The sky was blue and the water was blue because the water reflected the sky. And cutting through it like a shaft of divine light was the neck of that beast, the swan.

The beauty of a swan is in the way it displays itself, in the curve of its neck and the prim fold of its wings. I imagine it contemplating its own reflection. Its narcissism irritates me, though the precision – the success – of the moment cannot be understated. I can't help but feel that the swan knew precisely what he – she – was doing. I admit that I can't blame it for such faultless choreography. I am a slavish aesthete myself. I can only blame it for taking away my wife, for whose presence opposite me now I would gladly slash a hundred masterpieces.

★

Rape in classical antiquity exists on a spectrum, with 'necessary' at one end and 'glorious' at the other. Art historians are implicated in this crisis of interpretation, falling over one another to praise the harmony of form and composition. Since there's no neutral vocabulary, we choose to assume a position of moral relativity. We say that Zeus *seduces* Leda, we say he was her *lover*. To rape: to steal. From the Latin, *raptus*: seized, carried off by force. From which *seizure*, common in petit mal epilepsy. (I briefly confuse *petit mal* with *petite mort*. A different sort of dying.)

In this version of the myth, the swan doesn't caress the beautiful Leda with snowy white wings and return her to her husband, but seduces her so fully that she leaves forever. Instead of Leda taking the swan's head to her breast and smiling, her fingers languidly playing the neck as if to wring beautiful music from it, the swan was transformed into a sword and plunged by some force off-canvas into the body of my wife. She didn't bear me half-god children; she never came home at all. Instead of being silenced in a moment of pastoral bliss (the swan standing in for all those men, all that human lust, that the artists are too shy of depicting), she was *right in the middle* of a narrative, and the narrative was not just interrupted, it was brought to an abrupt close, taking my own with it. It's traditional in a Jewish home for sheets to be hung over the mirrors during the period of mourning. In my family we draped them over all the pictures too. When I asked my mother why, she replied, 'Just in case.' In the days that followed Leda's death I walked through my own house performing this ritual. In fact I would have liked to have drawn a sheet over my own head.

It's almost too embarrassing to mention the absurd nature of her death, given everything. So much so that, in fact, nobody mentioned it. I was constantly expecting to be asked about it. Isn't it odd, they might have said, or, I hate to bring this up but, well. And I would have raised my eyebrows, or shaken my head, I would have made them feel so ashamed for mentioning it. But nobody ever did.

I'm not religious, so I won't say that God took the form of a swan and stole Leda from me. They say there are no atheists in foxholes. That fear kidnaps us from the unbelieving world in which we lived. I've never been as afraid as that. I continue not to believe.

May 1988.

I'm sensitive. When I went to pick things for the salad the wind came and dragged across my face and left red marks. It also brought tears to my eyes. My mother noticed straight away. She said that I should try to become less sensitive. I rinsed the leaves in the kitchen sink. She said, why don't you wash your face, you'll feel better. I went upstairs and filled the basin with cold water. I ran my fingers along the welts on my cheeks and along my eyelids which were swollen and where the lashes stab outwards. After a while of sitting on the side of the bath watching a little brown cockroach walk one way and then the other on the cracked tiles my face was pale and smooth again. I came down and said hello to my uncle and my cousin, who had arrived to eat dinner with us. They were sitting quietly staring at the bottom of my cousin's foot. That was because he had a splinter in his heel. Then something disgusting happened. My uncle got down on his knees and sucked at my cousin's heel. It didn't do any good. He still had a splinter buried in there and he was also now humiliated. He couldn't meet my eye. I felt sorry for him. To have my uncle's moustache and his wet mouth on your heel like that. We ate the salad and there was a lot of loud conversation. To tell the truth, my uncle didn't get down on his knees and suck out the splinter from my cousin's heel. I only imagined it. I was 'playing tricks on myself'. Well, that's what my mother means about being sensitive. I imagine things and then I become disgusted that something like that could exist, even if only in my head. I wasn't crying when I came in from picking things for the salad. I was suffering from something called cold-induced urticaria. I know this because it happens every

*winter and the other children at school ask me what's
wrong with my face. I thought I should have an answer for
them so I looked it up in a medical dictionary, which is a
book that belongs to the library and which is too big to be
checked out. You have to look at the book there and then
go away again. I like to look at the names of the diseases
and late at night I imagine that I'm dying from them. I
haven't told my mother what cold-induced urticaria is. I
once asked her whether she knew that the clitoris was like
an iceberg and I didn't think she would ever recover. She
is an enemy of information. She prefers to spend her days
staring at mashed potatoes. When the sun goes down she
prays that it'll come up again. I don't pray because I know
the sun isn't coming up at all but instead that we are going
away and that there's nothing at all that we can do to
change it. When I am older I will buy a medical dictionary,
among other things.*

It's late in the day now and although I'm trying
to work, it is going slowly. I'm haunted by Robert
Provine. Not literally of course, the house couldn't
handle more than one ghost. To say nothing of my
nerves. And anyway he's still alive. Still, I'm imagining him behind me, looking over my shoulder. I
keep thinking of what he said once: that laughter
'can be of the ha ha ha variety or the ho ho ho
type but not a mixture of both'. That can't be right

surely? A schoolmate at Christ Church would hee hee inexhaustibly. Something to do with him having been a choirboy (not that it gave him a great sense of humour, just better breath control).

Art may rarely cause us to laugh out loud, but it's not unheard of. The methods are simple but time-honoured. Vulgarity, childishness, sex, toilet humour. The reason it takes us by surprise and makes us laugh is only because we show such ridiculous reverence for art. We view it in the chapels of galleries and in silence – alone or in pairs. This is the subject of a new course I hope to teach next year. I have been doing my best to persuade the university that there's merit in teaching the ridiculous. But recently I've found I've lost my sense of humour.

It's funny (funny 'weird', not 'ha ha'), the vocabulary used to describe laughter. A rhythmic, vocalised, expiratory and involuntary action – just like an orgasm – but it goes on and on. People die of it. They die of asphyxiation or cardiac arrest. Some underlying heart condition. Yes, an orgasm could kill a man with arrhythmia too.

Atonia. Collapse. These are the states we get our-selves into. The Greek Stoic Chrysippus is said to have died of laughter after watching a donkey eat the figs from his tree. He told his slave to bring the donkey a glass of wine with which to wash them down. Not very funny. I suppose you had to be there. That's something Leda and I would say with heavy irony and a smile. It was just one of our little jokes at other people's expense. I admit we were cruel on occasion but it was our way of being intimate – of becoming a team. We would stand on either side of the stupid person and simply encourage them to be stupid.

Last night while sleeping I felt the spectral presence of Leda's head on my chest. I woke to find it existed within me. It interlocked with each rib. I lay silently in pain, hardly able to breathe for fear of it lifting. I'm not mad, I know that the feeling was more than likely anxiety, and why shouldn't I be anxious? I'm suffering from the usual signs: weight loss, sleep disturbance, decreased socialisation. It's difficult to quantify just how *great* the decrease in my will to socialise has been. 'Grief is a generative and human thing,' I recall a psychologist saying in the early days. Yet I must admit I feel myself. Completely myself. It's just that I'm suspicious of every coming moment in case it sneaks up on me.

Who was it that eventually lost his mind after watching a horse being beaten? Every so often I remember this. Nietzsche, obviously. I can't imagine how one could possibly confirm the veracity of such a thing. Perhaps he was about to fall down mad

and a horse happened to be beaten in front of him.
This is the sort of thing I ruin dinner parties with.
If Leda were here – ah, but she isn't. So I'll simply
go on ruining dinner parties.

The funeral is generally considered to be the best
time to break down, if at all, isn't it? I could have
done with her at my side, that's the irony of it.
She, unlike me, would have known what to say
to the grasping mourners. They perched on the
arms of the overstuffed chairs with their mouths
moving apologetically. After everyone had left, the
proprietor of the place found me by the roses – like
them, rooted to the spot. We didn't say anything to
each other. I felt I'd said enough to last me several
years. Unfortunately he wanted to grieve with me.
I could see it happening in slow motion. He put
his hand on my shoulder like something washing
up on the beach. He was one of those men who
always looks to be leaking, or on the verge of it.
The slightest pressure and they erupt. He was also
completely undeterred by issues of personal space.

  Duddridge, that pygmy of a man, had been loiter-
ing dangerously close. I knew there was no escape
from the brunt of his adenoidal sympathy. He was
always a too-willing, too-appreciative, omnipresent
guest. He seemed to enjoy the funeral in the same
way he would a charity gala. At least there was no

piano in sight. He insisted – still insists – on playing at the drop of a hat. People applaud wildly when it's perfectly obvious that Duddridge is incompetent. Leda would at least roll her eyes in sympathy, though she was infuriatingly polite to his face – a trick I could never muster the enthusiasm for. I turned to face him by the mock Tudor dresser and was misted with a malodorous breath. I knew he'd said something but didn't care really what it was.

'I miss the fact that she knew how stupid everybody is,' I offered to him and then shrugged. 'I'll never find another woman like her.' I'd said something similar earlier in the evening and it had gone down well. Duddridge stared hard up into my face and seemed to chew something over with distaste before saying, 'You're lucky to be the widower of such a wonderful woman.'

'Jesus.'

'Seb, her loss inspires my honesty.'

'She was my wife for heaven's sake!'

'My God. You're right. Forgive me. Okay. Have a drink. Now we're getting somewhere.'

I offered my glass in silence and he filled it. His bloated face was purple and his eyes were straying independently of each other. He had been bleeding from somewhere and it had dried. I surmised that he had definitely been in love with my wife and I wondered whether – had she still been alive –

anything would have happened between the two of them. Leda had been tolerant of him. They used to speak late into the night. I hate telephone conversations and I hate miserable drunks. I felt she had been doing a duty in that cold kitchen of ours, sitting there. Until midnight sometimes. I had imagined her listening to him bore on and clenching her stiff fingers around a cup of tea and – I have to admit – I had felt relief that it wasn't me. But perhaps they had been intimate after all. Is it so unlikely? I found myself drinking the wine too quickly and staring at the bottom of the glass with ferocity. Was I about to get angry in that moment in front of Duddridge, by that dresser filled to bursting with the worst sort of crockery? No. It would be too dramatic. It would be exactly the sort of thing they all would have been waiting for. A scene. My temperament tested. I wouldn't allow it to happen. I simply patted Duddridge on his little sloping shoulder and stepped outside for a cigarette. The air bit into the flesh of my earlobes.

I am thinking about the rose that I gave Leda as an unimaginative birthday present. I collared a thin young man who was tethering pale stems to trellises and told him that it was my wife's birthday and he smilingly walked me (among dozens of other men on dozens of similar afternoons,

I imagine) to a rose called 'Birthday Girl'.

The Birthday Girl arched into sore-eyed flower and it was lovely and manageable, just as predicted by that man who knew roses. Hadn't I imagined with dumb optimism that it would die with Leda? And yet it survived. I neglected it for months but to no avail. I try not to look at it but still it blooms to spite me. I try not to see the flowers at the edge of my vision as I unlock the door every evening. Like sun spots. Or what they call *ocular ischemic syndrome*. Cotton wool balls drifting into the vision. I'd like to pluck the petals from their sockets and grind them underfoot, pink and buttering towards the centre. But it wouldn't do any good. I think of her eyes, threaded pinkly. And her forehead, how it would ridge in anger and in moments of sexual euphoria. Her face on the pillow, her gaze, direct and faintly mocking. Her hairline. The dark wisps that caught beneath her wrists and writhed on the bed sheets. What I wouldn't give to have my hands behind her knees now, lifting her towards me again. Her breasts flattened and spilling.

I remember the way Leda looked when she received the rose. She planted it. I gestured lazily to my wife and she got on her knees and worked to make something of it, something that was beautiful and true.

If I could only apologise to her I would apologise

for every moment I didn't make love to her, for every minute I let go to waste, for daring to break my mouth from her mouth. For what purpose? To breathe? If I could only stop my lungs from filling now.

June 1990.

I started to call Mother Petra about a week ago and in response she started to call me Daughter. It only sounded strange the first few times and now it comes naturally. Petra, I say, hand me that glass please. And as I'm filling it with water she says, 'Thirsty work, Daughter?' Although it might sound like she says it ironically, when I see it written down, I realise she actually says it with tenderness. That's the trouble with writing everything down like this. That's why I lock the diary up and put it under my bed. It's not that I want to keep secrets but that I want to be understood, and I know that if Petra read these entries she wouldn't understand. The only way I can make sure I'll be understood is to make sure I am around when my story is being told. That way I can correct myself if I misspeak, which I'm bound to do, because I'm only human. The other good thing about having Petra call me Daughter is that I can go for days at a time without hearing my name, that jarring sound, spoken aloud.

NOTE

Olaf found my diary and now says my name constantly. When we are down by the river he pins me down and says 'Leila, Leila, Leila'. It is worse than the other things that he does somehow. Still it's June and the birds are absolutely screaming with joy.

I can't work any longer. I find myself at the entrance to the park. It's the same park in which she died. The children are all at school and the weather is bad and the only people around are one or two desperate parents walking babies and a homeless man who sits with his body underneath a swing and his chin on the seat. Leda and I spent our first few walks in this park pointing at things, at birds and flowers, as if they'd been put there for us. However, we trod the same paths so often that I stopped finding it interesting. The smell of semen drifts up from the shrubbery, the specific stink of a species of flora that I've never got round to finding out the name of. It is, I realise, my first time entering the park since her death. I never understood the pleasures of walking the way that she did. I'm lazy. She wanted to get a dog, something loping and elegant, as generously limbed as she was, to keep her company. I refused because I don't like to volunteer to pick up actual shit with my hands three times a day. I can see now what the appeal had been for her though. I need something to do while I'm here – I can't amble along purposelessly. I feel paranoid and the skin under my shirt collar chafes every time I turn my head. Anyway I suppose it would have been Leda who would have picked up the shit. It's dull to have regrets. I'm just a person who has made the mistake of staying alive too long.

I sometimes accused Leda of being morbid because of the frequency with which she spoke of death, but she had been born into a family obsessed with mortality. If her lineage had been that of circus freaks then she would have been doomed to grow a beard or take up tightrope walking instead. The truth was that death was such an abstract proposition to me that the subject did bore me. Of course my parents died and I grieved in the usual fashion. I remember their funerals with some clarity. But the grief I had experienced was different, somehow, unreal. What luxury! A grief that allows buffet breaks.

I pause for a moment to look at the map. I know where I am but not where I'm going. The sun filters in a sickly way through the clouds as it tends to do in this country. Like a light bulb in a glass of milk. I clench my hands in and out of damp fists in my pockets. Anxiety has started to creep up over my neck and my chest like something spilled, scalding me. I can hear a couple only a few metres behind me and of course they're laughing – aren't couples always laughing? The laughter is loud, obnoxious. They want to prove how free they are, how unhindered by grim reality. I stare at a sign pinned to the map that is meaningless now thanks to rain blurring the ink that once formed words (some plea for a missing dog or a ban on barbecues, something that was once so important that someone felt it needed to be printed out and taken to the park and pinned to the map, but is now just an ephemeral blue-green presence, signifying nothing). Then I start to walk with great long strides down the left fork of the path and through the dark huddle of some overgrown trees away from the couple and I walk past a kicked-over bin and a bench and up the little hill and I'm there all of a sudden. In front of it. The lake.

I look up and then look away immediately. The policewoman has taken a seat beside me on the bench. She sighs and tucks a strand of hair behind her ear. She's come down to my level to make me feel comfortable. She's good at her job. She looks up at the park warden and smiles thinly and I can see the warden shaking her head. The warden points at me.

'He's a lunatic.'

'I'm dreadfully sorry,' I say.

'He fucking isn't.'

'All right, well, let's not get upset.' The policewoman makes a gesture to the park warden. The warden is swearing too much and the police don't like it when people swear. I see a fat-bottomed coot plunging head first into the grey water in the distance.

'Do they belong to the Queen?' I ask.

'What?'

'The swans. Do they belong to the Queen? Is that the trouble?'

'They belong to me! They belong to the park, I mean,' the warden corrects herself, looking to the policewoman for reassurance.

'Actually I think the Crown still retains all rights to mute swans,' the policewoman says, thoughtfully. She taps her pencil against her front teeth twice. 'Look, I do need to take down some information. Are you feeling okay? Are you on any medication?'

'No. Yes. I'm feeling all right.'

'And what about this lady's claim? Were you attempting to injure or kill the swan?'

'I don't know, really. I just—'

'He was throttling it!'

'Something overcame me.'

'Did you take the swan by the neck?'

'No. It was too quick. I sort of grabbed it. I think I got its neck in my hand but then it just got away.'

'I see. And why were you grabbing the swan?'

'There was this couple laughing behind me. I never meant to come this way.'

'He's a lunatic, Christ.'

'Seb?'

I turn my head. There are a few people standing nearby trying to see what the fuss is about. Among the gawping faces I recognise one peering down, and she says again, 'Seb? What's happening?'

'Anne?'

The phone rang often in the days following Leda's death but I had mostly ignored it. For some reason on this occasion I felt compelled to answer. Moved is the more precise word. My hand was moved by some force to pick up the receiver. I heard myself saying 'Hello,' that terrible sound. It was as if it echoed through catacombs before it reached my ears. It bounced from walls and gained some sick momentum. I said 'Hello' again to break the spell. The person on the other end of the line had said their hello at the same time and so we spoke over one another. Then I felt compelled to say 'Hello' once more, so as not to be interrupted. As I said it I realised it was ridiculous to say 'Hello' three times.

'It's Anne.'

'Oh, Anne. Sorry for saying hello so many times.'

'Just checking up on you.'

'I didn't hear you say hello, I wasn't trying to interrupt.'

It is Anne, a colleague and friend of mine and Leda's, a tutor in the art history department of something called Galleries (she couldn't care less for pictures or sculptures, but is obsessed for some reason with the buildings that contain them), who stands over me now. She intervenes as I sit there, staring into the grey lake. She tells the policewoman that I am the husband of the woman who drowned in the lake. She places a hand on my shoulder and guides me to her car, and then she drives me to my house, and I make us coffee. She sits across from me. I remember I once saw her eat an orange during a lecture and juice had run down her fingers. She had wiped her fingers on her scarf and I had looked away.

'Put the cup down,' I suggest, 'it's much too hot to drink.'

'I'm drinking it so as to have something to do with my hands,' she says, 'and so I don't have make conversation.'

'Ah,' I say.

'Oh, all right,' she says. She puts down the coffee and looks me in the eye and says, 'How are you doing?'

I say, 'Fine.' I smile, or rather I spread my lips across my face and do an impression of smiling, which has worked in the past.

'How's the course proposal coming along?'

'Very well.' I get up and look at the drinks cabinet. 'Oh yes. Very, very well indeed. Very well.' It's a Giorgetti walnut Canaletto cocktail cabinet with gold leaf. We bought it in Harrods and it was 'honestly the most beautiful thing' that Leda had ever seen in her life. I take out a bottle of rum and hold it aloft. 'RUM?' I ask.

'Why are you shouting?' Anne raises her eyebrows. She says that she will have some rum. I pour it into her coffee and mine. She says she is only having rum in her coffee to keep me company. I say that is fine even though I don't care whether she keeps me company or not. After we toast with our mugs I try and settle back on the sofa but Anne is staring at me curiously and a little fiercely.

'Seb, you can't murder every swan you see. You have to start thinking clearly.'

'Yes,' I say, inhaling the sweet steam through my nostrils. I briefly imagine lying on a bed of dead swans. The odour molecules bind and transmit their beautiful information upwards. I close my eyes.

I phoned the Samaritans a week ago. I was standing (or sort of leaning really) at the top of the stairs looking at the pattern of the wallpaper from very close up, which meant that with my myopia I was really seeing it for the first time – the grain, the way the colour of the leaves had been printed ever so slightly outside the line of the leaf. I said to the Samaritans that I 'couldn't cope' and they had said to me 'it sounds like you're having a really difficult time over there' and I had thought ah, but over where? On widower mountain where the winds blow icily over strange, hard fruits that used to be my eyes, my ears, my teeth, but that are now just marbles vibrating inside my skull waiting for a thaw to come? But all I said in response was, 'Yes, I am, thank you,' and the Samaritan said, 'Oh, you're welcome.'

I wake in the morning with eyes gummed and sore. There's a feeling I get when I've been drinking, a coldness that sets around my eyeballs. I've never been able to find a name for it, and nobody else admits to feeling similarly, but I have experienced it so many times that I know for sure it's a result of drinking too much. It is my skull making itself known.

I set about trying to leave the house and fail spectacularly. I end up at the kitchen counter with my hands over my head and bent forward as if I'm about to be taken roughly from behind. I've never explored that sort of thing properly. There was an evening when I was making love to Leda and she poked a finger noncommittally in that direction. I was terrified of enjoying myself so I screamed.

★

I've taken it upon myself to learn more about her. Even in death, why shouldn't I get to know my own wife? I'm unlikely to find a woman to interest me more. I take a trip to the library. It's the first time I've set foot in the place, even though I signed a petition to save it. There are three other people in there, and they all seem to occupy space on a spectrum from mildly to considerably insane. One old man resides within the vast expanse of a sports jacket. It sits approximately six inches above his head, which cranes forward on a thin brown neck. A hooked and spotted nose sits prominently in the middle of his face, with delicate glasses perched on top. He excites a great deal of phlegm inside his throat intermittently and reads *The New Yorker*, while his feet, which don't touch the ground, kick euphorically upwards so that the entire table ricochets, sending the paper flying towards his face, which distresses him, which in turn sets him to exciting the phlegm inside his throat. It is rhythmic and greatly alarming, and I wonder how on earth the fat man lying on the floor beside him can sleep.

There is nothing in the library remotely to do with Latvia. Perhaps on closer inspection it would be wiser to let the library die. I wonder if I can unsign a petition. Instead I go online. I type 'Latvia', and 'Latvian history'. I leave twenty tabs open while

I reheat a fish pie. As I spoon the mashed potato into my mouth I think of something that the anthropologist Johannes Fabian once said: 'Somehow we must be able to share each other's past in order to be knowingly in each other's present.' I finger my credit card, the hard impressions of each number.

I book my flight.

September 1990.
Usually I sit alone but today there was a new girl at school and she didn't know the rules about who has to sit alone so she sat opposite me. I was drawing birds in the margin of my book and she asked me to name them. I named as many as possible and then I stopped. I said, these birds don't have names because I made them up. They're just pretend birds. This one looks a little like a wagtail but I've given it a hooked beak. I was thinking of it being something like a parrot but kinder. She said, right. She chewed her sandwich. I thought, I've done it. I've made a friend. But then after lunch I guess the other girls told her the rules because she wouldn't make eye contact with me and when Ina said I had dirty knickers she laughed like haw, haw, haw. When I was leaving school I saw her sitting on the steps eating a little heart-shaped gingerbread. I can't explain the feeling that came over me very well, except that it felt that her fingers were clasped around my heart and that she was nibbling little pieces of it. I felt each tooth

mark in my chest. The crumbs fell into the pockets of my coat and onto the path in front of me and I imagined a huge crowd of birds descending from the sky and feasting on them. I felt hollowed out and strange. She looked up and caught me standing there, staring at her. I smiled. She said, go and kiss your cousin. Then she smiled back at me and I noticed that one of her teeth is missing, which is strange because she's too old to be losing her baby teeth. Maybe something horrible happened to her, too.

I leave the house while it is still dark. The chill catches my breath and releases it like powder slapped from a gymnast's hands. I catch the bus with people who seem awake, dressed, prepared. I feel somehow naked and ashamed. I'm carrying the largest carry-on bag that I can find: an old, curmudgeonly brown leather overnight bag that belonged to my father and that I insisted on using for trips much to Leda's annoyance (and despite the fact that she bought me a new wheeled suitcase that had a sleek red carapace, and which I nicknamed The Ladybird and doomed to a life in the attic). The leather of the handles has become shiny over the years from being handled first by my father's hands and now by mine. On the train to Gatwick the light pales and coolly silhouettes the branches of trees, thick mist rising among the legs of grazing horses. The sun eventually appears: red, completely round, severe and painful-looking, at the very edge of the sky. The country looks quiet and I am sorry all of a sudden to be leaving it.

On the plane people seem to arrive with full bladders and bowels – immediately there is a queue of six people for the toilet, which I am sitting close to. Their hovering presence at my elbow interrupts my concentration. An old lady leans heavily on my seat and says to nobody in particular, 'I'm too old for this,' and when nobody in particular pays any attention she shrieks, 'I'm ninety-two!'

'Perhaps you should think about going on a cruise next year,' I suggest, gently prising her blue little claws from my seat so that I can rest my head. She opens her mouth to protest but I can see that she's perfectly able to support her own weight so I simply nod and close my eyes to dissuade her from carrying on. I'm very tired but unable to sleep. Glancing upwards I make eye contact with a large man who has joined the queue for the lavatory. In turn he grins at me as if neither of us is aware of the stink he is doubtless about to produce. On the screen in front of me I see the blinking avatar that represents us in the air on our way to Latvia. It seems so close, so ridiculously close.

I knew Leda's family through stories, but I didn't know where to find them. Leda left Latvia in 1998 as a very young woman and, as far as I knew, only returned a handful of times in her twenties. She had come to terms with abandoning all that entirely for as long as I had known her. She was an Anglophile, and I encouraged her to embrace her identity as an adopted Englishwoman. It was easier for me. I felt confused and alienated by her foreignness. I preferred it as performance. The way she arched her hands while she was talking about some fruit that she had collected as a child and turned into a pudding.

I tried to find her family. I wanted someone at the funeral who I could talk to about the life she lived before I knew her. In that way I thought I could continue knowing her, could continue with the journey that we had started. I'd simply take a detour, I thought. I'd go backwards. But it was impossible. I hadn't listened closely enough when she'd spoken. I'd been looking at the shape of her hands. I scoured the house for information. I knew the vague pronunciation of the place she was from, but not how to spell it. I was distraught. Her friends simply shrugged. They did impressions of her, of how the syllables had sounded coming from her mouth, and I nodded. Yes, I said. That's how it sounded to me, too. In the end we went ahead with the funeral: we made the arrangements, we paid for several newspapers to carry an announcement. There was nothing else we could do. We wore black and huddled together. Had she kept in touch with her family, someone asked? I said, no. No. Definitely not. We were her family, one of the women in black said, her voice cracking in the middle.

Afterwards I took a box of photos down from the wardrobe and emptied them onto the bed. I sifted through belongings, attempting to sort them and to make some sense of things without her, to bring some sort of order to my own life. It was hard. I came face to face with a dress, still with the label on, that she had owned but never worn, had never even bothered to show me. I found a well-marked book that I have never heard of, let alone read. Worse still were the photographs of people I didn't know. Of men.

I knew that I owed it to her to continue. That I must resist the urge to sweep everything into boxes and then put the boxes onto a boat and set fire to it and push it into the sea. Maybe there was a young female relative or friend of a friend of somebody who would want to own a pair of her gloves, wear a ring, be told something of Leda's life? Since we didn't have children I felt compelled to sustain the narrative of her existence with somebody who knew her in a prehistoric way, who shared her blood. I unearthed another box, full of letters written in Latvian, so illegible to me, and sifted through to find something I could understand, such as a phone number, or – would the universe be so kind – an email address. Unfortunately I found no such thing.

However, underneath the letters I found something else: a large, unmarked, sealed envelope. I tried to open it neatly, feeling like a thief, but succeeded only in ripping the thing at an angle so that it burst from corner to corner. Inside were several envelopes addressed to L. Kauss, all at her old address, and postmarked from 1998 up until 2003. There must have been thirty letters in all, addressed in the same handwriting. Not one had been opened. I paused for a minute or two and checked my phone. This is how I communicate now: I don't write letters. I don't remember Leda writing them either. The items in front of me seemed fetishistic and I felt embarrassed holding them. (The strangest things embarrass me, Leda would point out early on in our courtship, and she was right, and still is. So much of art embarrasses me. I can't help but squirm when I imagine that an individual is attempting to express themselves, their right to hold a thought. I could never write a letter.) I sent a message to Anne, telling her what I'd found. In truth I was asking permission to claim these items as my own. To be told that they belonged to me.

I opened the most recent one first. Then I opened them all, and laid them on the bed in front of me like a jigsaw puzzle. They were signed 'Olaf'. There was a phrase before the name that repeated, too. '*Jūsu radinieks, Jūsu draugs.*' I typed it into my phone. '*Your cousin, your friend.*'

I have cousins, but they aren't my friends. I had supposed I might find a cousin, but not a friend. The word didn't ring true, somehow. If he were truly Leda's friend, wouldn't I have heard his name?

There wasn't much else I could glean from the letters. There were great chunks of text returned to me via an online translator with a robotic shrug, the odd word picked out but nothing to help me understand why Olaf had written for so long with no response, what he had to say to her for so many years that she had thought unimportant enough to ignore but significant enough to keep. The return address entered into Google Earth had me hover, buzzard-like, and swoop into a vast expanse of green that met the steely ocean with apparently nothing in between. There was nothing there: no roads, just forest, interrupted occasionally by tiny patches of cleared land and the white rectangles of rooftops separated by miles of dark treetops. For the first time I imagine Leda as a child who lived in a place that was like this. I had imagined her life to be only slightly dissimilar to mine: I had imagined shops and roads and neighbours and I was wrong.

I clutched a letter in one hand and my phone in the other, slumped in agony like Marat in his bathtub. My phone chirruped. It was Anne, to say she couldn't think that any harm would come of opening the letters. Well, of course she couldn't see the harm. There are some couples who lie awake at night telling each other intricate details of former lovers: who laid whose hands where, what positions they took, the size of historically examined breasts and penises. They do this, I imagine, in order to be titillated, but also in order to mutually forgive. But I've never wanted to play those sorts of memory games. Opening the letters was an act that I borrowed from somebody else. Not only had Leda been taken away from me, but I felt I was starting to lose myself as well. Grief is the aggressive displacement of the self from a known universe to another: you may choose to be the lover of somebody, or to follow a course of action that delivers you into the arms of another, but becoming their widower is an event that happens in spite of you. It sets off a chain of transformative actions that one finds oneself performing almost unconsciously, like a child. It's true that I've never felt so in need of care.

I opened the envelopes looking for the remains of an exquisite thing – despite having no intention of learning anything new about Leda, I chanced it. I wanted some existing thing to be shown to me: I wanted to be comforted. And here I am on a plane on my way to Olaf – her cousin, her friend – a person she never once mentioned to me, her husband. I am like a man possessed, I have never acted so fiercely from so little provocation. Each letter I ripped open seemed to somehow bring Leda a little closer to me than the one before. Each word I couldn't read was a word meant for her. The feel of the paper as I slid my thumb under the gummed lip of the envelope. The violent sound of an opening.

I listen to the hum of the engine, feel the cold breath of the air conditioning carrying a sigh from the front of the plane to the back. My newspaper lies abandoned on the tray in front of me. I can't read for more than five minutes without coming across a word that somehow looks wrong, my brain playing tricks on me. 'File' I read, and think, surely not? File?

The stewardess comes and hands me my plastic cup full of ice, my concentrated orange juice, strangely thick. In my hands I clasp the thing that lay in the last envelope of all – a lock of, unmistakably, Leda's hair.

June 1991.
It's my birthday. Petra promised me a party on the beach but when it got to be past eleven I went into her room and she was lying there awake with a pillow over her head.

It's my birthday, I said, in case she'd forgotten. I know, she said. Are we going to the beach, I asked. Take some money from my handbag, she said. There's pop in the fridge. Then she said, I didn't sleep very well.

I went downstairs and wrapped the bottle of pop in the towel. I did ask a few of the girls at school but they said that they couldn't come because they have horse riding on Saturdays now. It's unfair. I used to be scared of horses but now the only thing that scares me is the thing that's happening: I am stuck by myself and absolutely everyone else is out riding horses. Petra says that 1) I am scared of horses and that's why I never learned and now I'm too old to learn. And she says 2) I have to focus unless I want to be stuck here forever. I don't want that I said but then she interrupted and said 3) how many hours do you think there are in the day and how many days do you think we get a chance to live. I don't know what she's so scared of as the days are absolutely infinite and who cares how many we'll see.

I put the pop and my towel under my arm and took some money from Petra's purse. When I got to the beach two girls were there on their stupid horses! I don't think they saw me because they were having such a good time and throwing their heads back to laugh as if they were posing for a magazine or something. Neither of them are remotely funny so I can only assume that riding horses on the beach is an intensely good experience and I wish I'd known that when I was little so that I could have picked it. I never ever feel like throwing my head back to laugh when I'm painting.

I lay down on my stomach on my towel. I must have fallen asleep because after a while I felt something cold on the small of my back and I sat up quickly and screamed. Olaf was there. He had an ice cream and he was shoving it into the back of my swimming costume. Please, I said. It feels nice, he said. You like it. Please don't do that, I said. It's my birthday. He laughed. There was melted ice cream between his fingers and it caught in my hair.

I have hair down there now. Petra saw it yesterday when I was in the bath and she said, oh for God's sake.

There's no right way to grieve. I know that because so many people have told me, but also because I've done my homework. Rachmaninoff, for instance, suffered badly from depression brought on by his loss. For three years following the death of Tchaikovsky in 1893, he couldn't write a note. He recovered due in part to auto-suggestive therapy – one simply wills a thing to be and it is so. How sweet. However, in 1915 Rachmaninoff's dear friend Scriabin died and this time he reacted differently. For many months he gave concerts solely of his friend's music. What a lovely way to mourn; they asked for his repertoire and he retorted, 'Only Scriabin tonight.' I'd like to give other things thought, the university, for instance, the new course. The university will lose interest if I don't put something together, and quickly. Yet every evening I sit in front of my computer and I try to lead my fingers to the keys and instead they flutter above, and I must again admit: this concert, like yesterday's and that of the day before, will be for Leda. I imagine my audience getting restless. They whisper and start to chuckle nervously. The sound becomes intolerable. Hundreds, perhaps thousands, of people, uproarious and open mouthed.

There are many pathological causes of laughter: epilepsy (gelastic seizures), cerebral tumours, Angelman syndrome, strokes, multiple sclerosis, amytrophic lateral sclerosis (motor neurone disease). The name for uncontrollable and persistent laughter is, of course, Homeric. The etymology of Homeric laughter can be traced back to the *Iliad* – *asbestos gelos* – the unceasing laughter of the gods, who look down upon us to see our suffering and delight in it. The reason their laughter is without end is because our suffering is without end.

I have a pragmatic relationship with death, although this wasn't always the case. I think my own views about mortality were shelved, in fact, to accommodate Leda's. When I was a boy I often thought about dying, as Leda did, but not with fascination. I felt something more like revulsion. The idea that the thing I used to navigate the world – namely, my body – would one day refuse to work at all, and then rot, and then cease to exist entirely, made me feel physically uncomfortable to be trapped inside it. The sensation was as if I had been tied to the bed, and the urge to prove to myself that I was free was so strong that at times I would kick the bedcover completely away and would have to retrieve it from the middle of the room. Other times I stared in the mirror and opened my mouth as wide as possible, working against the muscles that move the two parts of the skull, held together by tissues both gelatinous and tough: the make-up of the thing that I called 'me', and carried around everywhere with myself. Eventually I began very benignly to consider suicide, just to get the damn thing over with – though, of course, nothing came of it. This feeling that mortality makes a prison of everything has basically evaporated, but not so entirely that I don't remember it on occasion: often when I catch or cut myself or stumble, the sudden terror springs like a cat from a high shelf, to scare the living shit out of me.

Do I think of Leda's last moments? Yes. I wonder whether she knew she was dying, or whether she thought she was just experiencing some temporary, horrible moment that would eventually be replaced by another moment, and so on and so forth, as usually happens – the seemingly banal reprise of existing.

I've experienced the deaths of both parents, and of one good friend. Each time I sat mutely with them as they articulated to me the ironic gift that is presented with the knowledge that death is approaching – that it is no longer frightening. I nodded and yet I thought, fiercely, and completely, 'That isn't true for me; that won't happen.'

When I first met her, I found myself in a position that I had never been in before. I wanted to know her. I devoured the information she gave me about herself in a way that I had only ever experienced previously with academic subjects. I found myself closing books, closing curtains, and devoting myself to the stories that she told. I listened to her talk about her day, wide-eyed, holding her feet and watching her face closely for signs of exactly how much she was enjoying the pressure I exerted with my fingers on the balls of her toes and on her heel. I listened to her say 'when' as I poured the milk into her cup and committed to memory the exact shade of her coffee. I did what all people do, I assume, and yet to me it was such a novelty, to not have to feign interest but to be truly enamoured with the information that spilled from her in short measures throughout the days.

Eventually something equally strange happened, although not until some time later. I started to become annoyed when some new fact surfaced. I became convinced I knew all there was to know, and when I was proved wrong, I grew angry. I accused her of fabricating things simply to prove to me that she was independent, that she existed without me and my knowledge of her. I refused to believe that she liked Verdi. How can you like Verdi, I asked her (sniffing the open milk carton to see if it had soured), since you're not an idiot? I interrupted a joke she was telling, by waving my arm between her face and the face of her friend and challenging the premise of the joke, which was that she had once lived in a flat in Walthamstow. I can't remember what the punchline was. In short, I acted badly, because the idea that I knew her was so central to my loving her. I knew her in a way that I knew nobody else. She, and everything she had ever done, and ever would do, belonged to me as much as it did to her.

September 1991.

There are lots of different ways to get home. For instance you can walk back along the beach with your shoes in your hands and your feet sinking into the wet sand, making suction noises as they lift up. Sometimes strange things are washed ashore or you might see wolf prints in the sand.

You see, walking on sand leaves a trail. You can walk back mainly by road. There are no paths as such on either side but there aren't many cars and so you can usually walk right in the middle, if you like, with the flat grass and the split forest either side of you. If you get home this way you can stop in and buy an ice cream or a bottle of pop. But the road is very flat and grey. You can see for miles. You can be seen for miles.

It takes a bit longer to walk back through the forest and things get in the way, trees that have been felled and great piles of wood, bright orange where the axe has landed and looking fluorescent and sore. You can follow a trail for what seems like hours and then it can disappear. It's not a trail but a fault of sorts. It's hard to get your bearings and it's impossible to know which way you're heading. There are animals above and below you. There are thin black snakes that shudder away from you or lie across your path, halfway through swallowing a toad. There are grey crows that sound the alarm in their throats and beat their wings. It's possible to get hurt, to fall and cut yourself. It's not safe. But it is a way to get home. It is a way to get home if you don't want to leave a mark, or if you are being followed, or if for some reason you just want to give the earth a chance to close around you, if you think that would be okay, for the ground to fall away, for the air to disappear out of your lungs like someone is pulling a fish hook out of your chest and for there to then be nothing at all.

I wait for the bus in Riga with a few other strays. The light is tempered by a saline fog. When the bus pulls up, I tell the driver the name of the nearest village. He sits and stares blankly back at me. I have to dig out the piece of paper from my bag where it is written down, and point at it. He nods. I pay him in exact change and find a seat on the right-hand side because I know that as we drive along the coastal road I will be able to get a good view of the sea. I am greedy now for the scenery, for the otherness of the place, and there is nothing more foreign to me than the sea.

A woman and her son get on the bus shortly after me, but to my surprise she speaks to him for a moment and then kisses his head and smilingly withdraws. The child can't be more than nine or ten. His feet hang from the seat and dangle in mid-air. He waves at his mother noncommittally as she leaves. She doesn't even wait for us to pull away. I watch her retreat through the glass doors of the bus station, swinging a bag onto her shoulder.

The city thins quickly. Many of the buildings are shuttered and in disrepair. A thought from earlier, that there is something of the Wild West about the place, crosses my mind again. The graffiti is half-hearted and ugly. Eventually we are on a motorway with no scenery at all. We cross through miles of nothingness into land that is pastoral, and then wild.

The sea is waiting through the trees for me to see it, in flashes of silver and blue. I feel the jolting shift as my brain tries to collect and order the information. I'm a little afraid.

After a couple of hours I am the only one left on the bus. I wonder where the boy is now, whether he is already sitting in front of a breakfast that somebody has cooked for him. We are now travelling along a straight yellow road that cuts through endless pine trees. Everything has been swallowed up by the dark forest. The road shimmers with a false wetness up ahead. The sun has broken through the fog and the light is tender.

Imagine for a second the old trope of a cartoon character leaping onto a stool and pulling her skirt up around her knees to avoid a mouse. Imagine for a second that the mouse is made of Leda's hair and that the screaming cartoon character on the stool is me, discovering it at the bottom of an envelope. That's as clear as I can be about the hysteria that rose in me when I found it. Although outwardly I am a man sitting slightly stiffly in his seat, ever since then I have been clutching my apron and screeching at the top of my lungs.

I'm going as far west as it's possible to go. I have studied the map, there's no stone left unturned. I am a planner, I always have been. It drove Leda mad. The tension starts to ebb away but I still feel its grip on my neck and shoulders, and know that it won't leave me entirely until I am where I am scheduled to be, at the time I had scheduled myself to be there. For this reason I carry on staring forwards, as if by sheer will alone I could conjure up the correct stop. It seems impossible that anything resembling a village could exist here. The road goes on and on, and the breaks in the trees give away nothing. There is no trace of anything except forest. I even doubt the existence of the sea.

I arrive at the house, although it is unclear how I should approach it. There is one large house which is turned away from the road and surrounded by a veranda, and around it are smaller buildings scattered like picked-clean bones. There is a flurry of birds that excite the trees above me. Apart from that there is no noise of any sort, and no answer when I knock on the door. I try to call the number that I have for Agnes, the woman who owns the place, but there is no reception. I put my bags down and walk around to the back of the house where there are large glass doors that have been slid slightly open. I rap my knuckles against the glass. There is no answer. I slide a door open and say 'Hello' loudly. Suddenly there is a flurry of activity behind me. Agnes appears and seizes my shoulder. She pulls me back out of the house and speaks quickly and sharply to me in Latvian, her temperament completely indecipherable. I shake my head and say, 'Sorry, no Latvian, only Russian,' and she stops for a second, her mouth still open as it moves to form around a word. She changes her mind and snaps her fingers, grinning widely as she realises who I am, and I understand that she had somehow mistaken me for an intruder. Then she says in Russian, 'You sound younger on the telephone. I was expecting a young man.'

Agnes walks slowly around the rooms, pointing at things and naming them. I can communicate perfectly well in Russian, but we are playing a game. She says the word in Latvian first, deliberately, and staring me straight in the eye. Then she says the English word if she knows it, and raises her eyebrows questioningly if she doesn't. This means that I should say the English word. When I do, she inevitably laughs. She repeats it and then shakes her head and laughs, as if it is the most idiotic thing she has ever heard. I laugh too and shrug. I am making a show of apologising for my language even though I don't see anything particularly wrong with it. I want her to like me and this charade is simple and fun and makes me feel at ease. I know what I have to do and I know what she will do before she does it. This is good. This means that I have no unhappy surprises.

In the kitchen she points at a substantial pair of
scissors hanging from a metal hook above the
counter. They are curved gracefully upwards like
the neck of a drinking bird.

'*Putnu šķēre*,' she says. Then she looks at me
expectantly.

'Scissors,' I say. She shakes her head but this time
she doesn't laugh.

'Scissors, yes. I know scissors. But these are for.
You use for ducks and ham. What is this word?'

'Oh,' I say. 'Meat. Meat shears.' I turn the words
over in my head. I knew such things existed but
I had somehow never come across them. So this
is a house with meat shears hanging from a hook,
I think.

Upstairs I unpack my suitcase and lay my clothes
in the dresser under the window. Rain is falling
doggedly outside. I go to the bathroom mirror and
look in. My suit is wrinkled and I need a shave. I
turn the tap on and the sink fills with hot, sulphuric-
smelling water. I raise a handful of it to my mouth
and dip my tongue in. It tastes the way it smells: like
rot. Agnes must have some drinking water, I think.
I'll ask her for a bottle to last me until tomorrow. I
wonder why the water is rotten. Where is it coming
from? A well? I dip my shaving brush in the water
and grind the bristles into the soap. The lather rises

reluctantly. When I have finished there is a blob of it on my cuff and for some reason I have to resist the temptation to taste that, too.

There is a knock at the door. Agnes stands there with an assortment of items in her hand. She smiles and comes into the room although I have made no movement to invite her in. I suppose I have just arrived, and the ownership of the space hasn't been properly handed over, psychologically speaking, from Agnes to myself.

She drops a pile of maps on my bed, and then looks around for a place to plug in the other object, which appears to be a clock. It flashes 00:00 in red digits, needing to be set. She taps her wrist and I unbuckle the watch from my own wrist and give it to her. I don't wear a watch to tell the time with, so for all I care she can keep it. I wear it for purposes of vanity, and there is nobody here to admire it. I bought it one afternoon in a second-hand shop that I had been dragged to by my girlfriend at the time in a small town by the sea. I forget the exact location, only recalling that things weren't going so well with this girl and that I was bored out of my mind. When I saw the watch, I bent over and picked it up and held it close to my face. It was nondescript, I suppose, handsome but fairly small. I liked the way it looked on my wrist anyway when I laid it across.

I was twenty-five and I had never worn a watch in my life. Since that moment I can barely remember more than four instances when I have removed it, other than to wash. There was something about the ritual of taking the watch off and laying it on the bathroom shelf in the morning before I showered, and fastening it again once I was dry, that I took to immediately. I remember the girl I was with had said that it was a woman's watch. She had said that it was a watch that was designed to be worn by a woman.

Now Agnes looks at it while she sets the time on the alarm and tunes the radio to a local station. A song comes on that she recognises. She holds out her hand as if to take mine in it. I raise my eyebrows in what I think is a good-humoured manner and shake my head wildly. She wants to dance, of course. She is attempting to forge a friendship. I don't want that under any circumstances. Suddenly Agnes is dancing, in an ironic way, in front of me. Her hair (mostly grey – although she is only a few years older than me – and thick as a horse's) falls in front of her face. She throws her head back and laughs. I laugh politely too but I fervently hope that she will bring the present festivities to an end and leave me alone. Instead she goes through the radio stations, pausing at each one and nodding significantly at me.

'Yes,' I say, 'very good.' Jesus Christ, I think. The

woman is clearly starved of attention out here. I must be the first person from outside the village she's seen in months, maybe years. What have I dragged myself into? But then I remember I know nothing about her. She's probably just being friendly for the sake of politeness, and in turn can't wait to get back to her own business downstairs. Before leaving, she points at the maps.

'You cycle?' she asks, in Russian, miming the action frantically, with her tongue for some reason hanging out of the side of her mouth like a dog's.

'God, no,' I reply. I shake my head and turn the corners of my mouth down, just in case. I haven't been on a bike since I was fifteen years old and I'm certainly not about to climb on one now, here. She shrugs.

'You walk, then. The sea...' She pauses and searches for the words. She puts her fingers together as if about to crush a bug.

'Close?' I venture.

'Yes. Very close.' The two fingers come together, and the invisible cockroach is extinguished. Satisfied that I have all the information I need, she walks backwards out of the door, shutting it behind – or rather, in front of – her.

May 1992.
Petra asks, why don't you invite some of the girls from
school round? She says, we have a big garden, I can make a
cake. What's wrong with you, Daughter, she asks, and puts
her hands under my chin and lifts my face so that I am
looking at her. I close my eyes and shake my head. If you
want, she says, I can call your uncle and ask him if you can
go over and play with Olaf and his friends. He has friends
to spare and our door doesn't feel a single knock all summer
long. Aren't you lonely, she asks? My spine goes cold. I'm
just practising my music, I say. And I'm learning to draw.
It's important for me to learn the techniques or they won't
consider me at the best schools. I'll be rejected and I'll have
to stay at home and work at the market. My teacher has
given me special assignments. I have more homework than
everybody else because I'm cleverer, I protest. As I speak
I can hear my voice climb hysterically. And anyway, I say,
trying to stop the trembling in my throat, you know how
sensitive my skin is these days. Going outside irritates my
face. Petra stares at me with her hands on her hips. Then
she goes to the window and yanks the thin yellow curtains
as far to the sides as they will go, threatening to pull the
hooks from the rail. Then she props open my window. For
your complexion, she explains, twitching her thin eyebrows.
It's important that you grow up to be beautiful as well as
good. The way she says 'good' is as if it is a dirty word.
Eventually she leaves me alone. In the mirror I look at my
face. It's true that I am more good than beautiful.

Although the department has been very encouraging about my trip, I think it wise to persevere with my plans for instating the new course while I'm away, to keep the momentum going. I set up my old laptop on the desk that also functions as a dining table. Agnes has told me that I must feel free to use her kitchen, but there is also a working hotplate and a little fridge and kettle in my room. I bought provisions in Riga, including potatoes, eggs and a bottle of wine. I was needlessly austere in my choices, imagining, I suppose, that I would be arriving to a different sort of a life – that although in my day-to-day existence I regularly buy pomegranate seeds that have been removed from the hull of the fruit, and fish that have been gutted, descaled, cleaned and filleted (while I stand uselessly by, rotating an artichoke in my hand just for something to do), here I would somehow be content to eat a hunk of bread and carry a hard-boiled egg in my pocket on long walks through the unfamiliar landscape. But Riga is a capital city like any other, and in it was a supermarket like anywhere else in the world, with exotic items and familiar ones. I had to force myself to ignore the confectionary, of which there was so much, the marzipan-filled chocolates and bottles of sweet wine. While I was waiting for my six white eggs to be rung up I looked mournfully at the over-full baskets of my neighbours.

I sit down and send an email to Anne, to tell her that I have arrived safely. Almost immediately a reply appears in the browser.

'Great. Keep safe,' she writes. 'Everyone thinks you've taken annual leave to write a book. What's the weather like? Have you met him?'

I had no telephone number for Olaf. When I searched the White Pages, a dead number was returned. Instead I wrote to him, on a postcard, to minimise the embarrassment I felt at not being able to fill a page, at not knowing how to talk to him or even how to begin. I informed him of the date of my arrival in the country and that I would make a brief call, to drop off a couple of Leda's things. I didn't give a return address. I couldn't shake off the feeling that I was meddling in something that didn't concern me. I talked to Anne about it but nobody else. I kept the letters by the bed and looked at them at night. To say I read them would be incorrect. To me they were hieroglyphics. But I spoke each word in my head, as I thought it might have sounded. I attributed meaning to each of them. And I kept the lock of hair in my inside pocket. From time to time I remembered it was there and felt it burning like a hot ember through the fabric and onto the skin of my chest. I just need now to meet him, to have him say the magic words that will lift the veil. Why did he keep writing?

Agnes has absconded and there doesn't seem to be anyone else living in the house. The silence is so strange to me that I find myself jumping as the door shuts behind me. I know there is a shop within walking or cycling distance, from what Agnes has told me, and I decide that it would be a nice gesture to pick up some alcohol – the sort of gesture that will make her think well of me. It's important to make a good impression and I can't trust my spontaneous actions to do that for me. Gifts are less likely to be misinterpreted.

The shop is small, with a broken window that has been repaired with a gaudy patchwork of striped tape and circus posters. After a moment's hesitation I push the door handle. It isn't that I am afraid to go in and make a fool of myself by speaking the language badly, or not speaking it at all. Similar actions in my own country, in my own part of the city, come more easily to me only by virtue of repetition. That I don't hang on to every door handle for a fraction of a second longer than necessary, I think of as brave. I think myself an extrovert, a person full of his own self-worth, egotistical even, due to the fact that I can walk and talk each day – the fact that I'm not paralysed with fear by every second that demands action of me.

Inside I pick up bread and a bottle of water. I stop in front of the cold cabinet to consider the cheeses. Fortunately I can do this without being scrutinised because there is a very old man in front of the till, chatting to the tired woman who stands behind it. He makes an observation or joke and then turns and ponderously makes his way to collect some other item. I stand beside him and he turns to face me and says something loudly. He laughs with his eyebrows raised high on his head. I say, 'I'm sorry, I'm English.'

'English. Where from? Washington?'

'London.'

'Ah, London! Big Ben! Margaret Thatcher!'

Without understanding what I'm doing I raise one finger and pass it along my throat. 'Dead.'

'Dead?' He looks horrified. Then he shrugs. He comes to terms with the information. 'Dead. Ah.' He raises his bag, full of beer and dog food, and turns to leave.

I feel terrible for having been the one to tell him. I put my goods on the counter and then try to pay with a handful of coins. The woman taps the tray in front of her and I put them down. She uses one finger to flick them one by one, to make sure I'm not swindling her, I think. And then she says, 'Okay. Goodbye.'

*

A wooden table and chairs sit outside the house. The chairs are a little rotten and have thick cushions of cobweb slung between each slat. I dust a seat off, sit down and open my book, waiting for Agnes. By the time she returns I am unwittingly hunched over it with my face inches from the pages, trying to make out the words in the failing light. Agnes looks at me with a strange expression on her face, something like bemusement or maybe irritation. She leans her bike against the house and lets herself in, the door slamming with a terrible bang that seems not to affect her at all. She comes out after a few minutes with a large mason jar, holding three tealights and a box of tapers, and deposits them wordlessly on the bench. I thank her but she carries on into the house as if she hasn't heard. Although I taught myself how to say please and thank you in Latvian before I arrived I might as well not have bothered since nobody other than children seem to care about or use the words. So far everybody here has been rude in a way that I am scared of inadvertently being. I've trained myself my entire life to act in opposition to the cold, exhausted way that interacting with other people made me feel, and here I am in a country surrounded by people who I feel could be my family in that sense. Only in that sense. There is a large stone urn next to the entrance to the house which is filled with cigarette butts. I imagine it with strawberries and herbs growing in it. In the kitchen Agnes sings along to a mournful song, with lyrics that I can't understand.

Leda spoke Latvian in front of me only once. We had found out that she was pregnant. I held her very tightly in my arms. I thought that she looked wild in that moment, close to hysterical, although we both smiled and had tears in our eyes. We were happy but I pinned her arms to her sides with that embrace. She pulled away and there were strands of her hair that had stuck to her high forehead with sweat. She looked up at the sky and said a few words in Latvian. I wish I could remember the phonetics of what she said, even a vague approximation, so that I could try and find out the meaning now. But unfortunately all I remember is having been afraid of not understanding her, how foreign she seemed to me then, and how foreign the situation was, in which there was something stirring between us, loosening the layers of the woman that I loved, and that I was powerless to stop. I needn't have worried because three weeks later Leda had the baby aborted. We had had an argument that lasted all night. I don't know now what it was about, only that the tension filled the house from wall to wall and stuck us helplessly in place like specimens. It was one of those nights where the sun rises without your permission. I went to bed and lay face down and listened as she dialled the number and booked the appointment. I lay with the cold light creeping over me. The odd sound of her voice like a stranger's in the hallway. Had we agreed that she should make the call? I can't remember now, only that she did.

When the time came for her later that week to catch a taxi to the centre in Archway to have the termination done, we had made up. We were as in love as ever. Nevertheless, we made breakfast and showered and called for the taxi. We didn't discuss it, although sometimes at night before we slept I could tell that she wanted to. I'm not immune to every nuance. I could feel the electricity of the conversation before it had had a chance to begin. It crackled in the air. And then because we had been silent for so long, we just gave up and slept. It was so much easier for Leda to sleep. She would go to bed in the middle of an argument as if the act of fighting had somehow infected her and made her ill. I have not always been able to sleep. But Leda could lie unmoving for hours. She could have slept if the world had cracked open. If hell had risen up to meet us, and everything that was in it, Leda could have slept.

When Agnes reappears, I offer her some cheese and she accepts. She asks me about my plans, and I tell her about Leda and about the letters from Olaf. She chews thoughtfully and then offers to help me. She says that she knows everyone in the village and that everyone knows her. When I tell her the name of Leda's cousin, she nods and says that yes, she knows him. She says that sometimes he comes to the house after he has been hunting, to clean and prepare the dead animal. Agnes is a trained butcher, from a family of butchers, but she abandoned it as soon as her father died in order to run the guesthouse, though only one room (the one I am staying in) now remains functional.

'My father wanted a boy,' she says, her lips slightly stained with wine and flickering orange in the candlelight. 'He was very sad with a girl. But now it doesn't matter.'

Olaf gives Agnes some of the meat if she helps him to butcher it. She is, by her own account, more adept at it than anyone else. She stands suddenly and beckons and I follow her towards one of the smaller buildings. Inside is a chest freezer filled with various cuts of dark meat, wrapped in cling film and bits of what looks like muslin. They remind me of discarded dolls in shrouds. She tells me to help myself, and says that she herself is practically a vegetarian now.

'I like cheese,' she says, 'and wine.'

'You should have been born in France,' I say, idiotically. Agnes smiles and nods.

'Perhaps, yes,' she says, 'but this is my home instead.'

I feel embarrassed and I'm very aware of the cold, damp smell of the shed and the hum of the freezer. Agnes slowly closes the lid and we walk back out into the mosquito-studded evening. 'What day will you meet Olaf?' she asks.

'Tomorrow,' I say. 'He's expecting me tomorrow.'

'And you've never met?'

'No.'

'I'll make a nice dinner,' she suggests.

'Oh, you don't have to do that.'

Agnes looks confused.

'I mean, thank you,' I say. 'That would be very nice.'

I fry potatoes and eggs, salt them heavily and eat while staring out of the window, the cold compress of a hangover settling over my forehead. I check for emails from Anne or my colleagues; inexplicably, I haven't heard back from them following my last missive. It is cold in the house. I boil water for tea and take a shower in the stinking water while keeping my eyes and mouth firmly shut lest it worm its way inside me. When I emerge, Agnes is on her phone. Seeing me, she gestures excitedly for me to come to her. I'm rooted to the spot: she mouths the word 'Olaf'. Then she puts the call on speakerphone. Suddenly the room is full of a thunderous male voice. It is him – and although I haven't a clue what he might be saying, I listen to it like a convert receiving a speech from his religious leader. Indeed, we stand without moving in front of the phone as it acts as a transmitter for this heavenly thing that is Olaf's voice, and he talks and talks without end. He sounds slightly older than me, perhaps, and I am able to picture him then as a person within a body that has continued to age, like mine; while the idea of Leda has been removed and placed under a glass cloche, Olaf has been fully fleshed and presented to me. He is a person with whom I can begin to get acquainted, and continue to know. For some reason I feel as if I might be sick. I stand like a frightened child called on to do some horrible pantomime and Agnes looks at me curiously while talking into the phone in garbled Russian, stabbing the air between us with a declamatory index finger as if to say, 'Look! Look! Look!'

It is hard for me to specifically recall Leda talking about how she came to leave her home country. At most, I can faintly recall her doing an impression of her mother, who was equal parts pushy – insistent that her daughter be the best at school and that she apply for the best (the most foreign-sounding and therefore the best) universities – and narrow-minded. I'm certain that she visited her daughter only once in England, while she was at Chelsea. She stayed in the cramped room that Leda rented and refused to venture further than the college, which she admired. She talked nastily of how busy London was, how unhygienic, and each morning she would wake her daughter by making her investigate the contents of her handkerchief, which, Leda had to admit, were grey. I can so nearly conjure the image, the sound of Leda as she exaggerated her mother's accent and looked down her nose at some dinner plate or other – and yet the memory fades into vague caricature, for do I imagine she hunched as she spoke, or that she held her folded hands in front of her like a Victorian nanny? Am I simply amassing the hundreds of impressions that I have seen people do of Mother, each barely distinguishable from the next even in the enacting, let alone years later? What is going on in my hippocampus? If only I could process thoughts the way I chew meat, pausing to run my tongue over every fibre. Oh yes, I can see the impression clearly enough, but I am also able to 'see' the silver menorah stolen from my grandmother as she slept – despite the fact that I was still latched to the breast at the time, and, furthermore, despite it having been stored in a cupboard and not having seen the light of day for twenty or more years, deemed 'too special' to use.

It's debatable how much of memory is fabrication. I believe there's been research done to refute the idea that these two things come from the exact same place. But this notion speaks to my sensibilities. It will be a sad day for me if they manage to pinpoint the exact split. How wonderful to me to imagine a flush system that panders to our need to *own* and to *order* and to *collect* events and occasions as if they belong to us. As if we are anything but slack-jawed witnesses to the terrific road traffic accident that is the world, occurring.

January 1993.
I wish I had a sister. Or a female friend. Petra says, 'Not even the Devil knows where women sharpen their knives.' She thinks it's making me strange to spend so much time alone. When I come home from the library she is curt with me and makes little jokes about what I have been doing there. The jokes are hard to understand because they consist of her doing an impression of somebody at the library and then laughing. She puts a magazine up to her face and reads the words very closely. When I try and speak to her, or laugh a little bit – to persuade her that the joke has been successful and can now come to an end – she shushes me, with one long finger to her lips. She makes an exaggerated expression of concentration and this is supposed to be funny. Petra acts as if there is a live TV audience present at all times. It's as if one side of the house is not there at all, but is just a curtain to be lifted so that our

*performances can begin. When my mother isn't at home
the audience members are very quiet and respectful. They
cough into their handkerchiefs and so on. It's good to
know that they're there, but I wonder what they make of
it when I pretend to be married to various things around
the house, or that time last week when I sewed stones into
the pockets of my coat.*

*She makes me summarise what I have learned. Some-
times I don't learn anything. I read and read and all I learn
is that rich Russian women throw themselves under trains.*

The day of my meeting with Olaf arrives with thin
rain and I wake from a night of relentless dreams that
toss me hotly from one side of the bed to the other.
The smell from my nightclothes is alien and when I
undress I throw them into a plastic bag and tie a tight
knot in the handles. Even the rotten water comforts
me as I work it under my armpits and between my
toes with a cracked sliver of soap. I have hours to
kill before dinner but I tidy my papers hysterically
rather than do anything worthwhile. I email Anne
and the others, but I embarrass myself with too little
thought and too many ellipses, signifying nothing.
He's going to sit across the table from me, I think.
Once again I stand at the window watching the sky
contort itself with rain clouds. I hold Leda's lock
of hair in my fist. It is dark and glossy and weighs

heavily somehow, as if it is a rope, as if it is a thing that connects a ship to the land, as if something is straining at the other end of it.

Agnes is very proud of herself, standing over a steaming pot in the kitchen. I hover uselessly. She fusses around the room and keeps asking me whether or not I eat certain things. She says, 'Pork?' and I grimace and nod, which I think is perfectly reasonable sign language for 'reluctantly'. She stands with a knife dangling from one hand and the other on her hip and says 'Yes or no?' irritably. I say yes. Then she says mushrooms, then she says onions. I stand in the middle of the room and stare at her. Of course I eat onions, I think. Ridiculous. Who doesn't eat fucking onions? But I smile and nod politely. She's starting to get on my nerves. I imagine the immaculate impression I will do of her upon my return. Then I go back upstairs to my room and shut myself in. I manage to tidy up a few things and read a bit of an American crime novel that I found the evening I arrived, while I was searching for a power socket behind the bed. Every so often she comes upstairs and bangs on the door with her fist asking for help, either chopping vegetables or laying the table, as if I'm a young relative come to stay with her for the summer rather than a paying guest. I find myself schlepping up and down the stairs, half from nervous energy and half in response to Agnes's demands. She listens to the same radio station at an inexplicable volume. It plays some music but it seems to be predominately a phone-in show. Occasionally Agnes will pause in whatever she is doing in order to give it her full attention, and then she will translate the opinions of the listener for me, broadly, as either those of an idiot or those of a considered individual like herself. I can't focus my attention on what she is saying. I keep thinking of, anticipating, the arrival of the man who is on his way through the forest to meet me. By the time the water has started to boil I've created a monster from him. A titan. A beast.

And yet Olaf crawls from the envelopes that I opened back in the real world and is – all of a sudden – standing in the kitchen somehow, with his hands in his pockets. A man, stooped slightly, with a downturned mouth and a greasy coat.

We shake hands and he considers me from a great height. Actually he is probably only five inches taller than me, but it seems as if I'm staring into the snows of a mountain. I say his name two or three times, and Olaf nods, as if encouraging me. He sits on a chair and starts to smoke a cigarette. I watch Agnes poke the water, which has formed a grey scum around the fist of the ham.

'Do you recognise him?' Agnes says.

'No. I've never met him before in my life.'

'Does he look like your wife?' Agnes stands

between us and looks from one face to the other. She smiles and wipes her hands on her jeans. I can tell she's having a good time.

'You have a similar mouth,' I say to Olaf. He looks up at me and his eyes look more like a cow's than a man's. His eyelashes are long and underneath them the pupils pool like they belong to an injured animal. But they don't look anything like Leda's. Olaf smokes his cigarette.

I feel as if his skin is on my skin. I feel as if the bristles swimming in the soup belong to him. I can barely stand the smell of the meat in the room. I am lying about his mouth. Or rather, one minute the shape of it is familiar to me and the next, as it puckers around the filter of the cigarette, it is grotesque and alien. Agnes pushes at my lower back, encouraging me to sit down on a chair opposite Olaf that angles outwards. I must sit down. If I don't sit down I will fall down. I sit.

'Tell me about yourself,' I say. We are speaking in Russian and it feels wrong in my mouth. There is a beat before Olaf moves to answer me and I wonder if I've said the sentence correctly. But eventually, inevitably, he replies, 'What would you like to know?'

What would I like to know? Everything.

'What do you do?' I ask.

'Oh, I don't know.'

'You don't know. I hear you hunt.'

'Ye-es. Everybody hunts.'

'Not me. I've never hunted anything before in my life.'

'I will take you.'

'That's okay,' I say. I shrug. Agnes uses a large fork to remove the flabby meat from the pot. She places it on a board and carves it and then puts the board with the carved meat in the middle of the table between Olaf and me. He smiles at me and uses his forefinger and thumb to select a thick slice. I can see he has gaps between his teeth. He nibbles the meat in a delicate way. He eats like a prince. For several minutes the room is silent. I ask him if he lives nearby and he says that he does. I ask if it is the house he grew up in, meaning the house where Leda may have been as a young girl, because the thought of this excites me. Perhaps I could visit, I suggest, meaning that perhaps I could visit it as if it were a museum and silently parade through the rooms with my hands behind my back. I ask him to describe the furniture, to name the trees outside. I want to put my face between his hands and inhale the smell of Leda's life: the polish on the arms of chairs, the crushed needles of the pines, the rough fur of dogs playing under tables. If I put my ear to his hands will I hear her voice, rising up a staircase, singing? If I put my mouth there will I be able to whisper to her, will I be able to speak? I lean forward over my plate, my hand shaking as it reaches for the glass. My teeth get in the way and I crash the wine into them. Olaf seems to have lost the power of speech and eats methodically instead of answering my questions.

'Excuse me,' I say, and he looks up startled from his plate. All the while Agnes leans back in her chair, dipping hunks of bread into her plate and sucking the wet brown parts off as if she were watching a show on television.

'It's not the same house,' Olaf says eventually. He looks at me for a long time and says, 'It's not the same house. At all.'

'Where is the house Leda was born?'

'I didn't call her that,' Olaf replies. 'I called her a different name.'

'Is that right?'

'Ye-es. There was nobody here called Leda.'

'What did you call her?'

'That's private,' Olaf says. He has tears in his eyes suddenly. He's holding the fork in his fist and his eyes are shining. 'That's not your business.' There are sweet ribbons of fat in the meat.

'I don't think it's private,' I say. 'After all, she was my wife.'

'His wife. He does not know even his wife's name,' Olaf says, to Agnes. He says something in Latvian and shakes his head. Agnes pauses and then whispers a reply, something conciliatory. I stare impatiently from one to the other. Finally Olaf says, quietly, 'Leila. Leila. Leila.'

'Nonsense,' I say. 'You're mistaken.' I halve and quarter a hard little potato.

'She was Leda in England, yes, married to you. But her name was Leila. We knew her as Leila. My cousin's name was Leila.' He punctuates each horrible sentence by tapping the tines of his fork against the side of his plate. He has composed himself and is looking at me with two eyes like pennies left out in the rain. I eighth the potato. I sixteenth it. I mash it into the liquid that pools around the meat, into the yellow fat and into the grey water.

Olaf smiles blandly. 'All stories have a beginning.'

I am somewhere else. I am swimming in an enormous pool and I cannot touch the bottom or see where it ends. I butter bread and then put it to one side. I pass a morsel of meat from one side of my mouth to another. I nod politely and answer when Agnes pushes me to talk about myself or my life in London, which both she and Olaf are interested in for different reasons. However, I am afraid. I am afraid of the thing that Olaf has told me. How can I not have known that Leda was once Leila, that the woman I shared my life with had been named not after the woman most beloved of Zeus, but after – what?

Perhaps it is a small thing. Perhaps it is nothing.

I imagine her cutting out her name as if it were a paper doll and putting it in an envelope. There are a hundred questions I want to ask Olaf but I don't. He asks me things instead. How did she die, he asks? I tell him and Agnes laughs out loud. I thought it meant something, I want to say, but it meant nothing. Instead I keep quiet. After a polite drink I plead a constriction in my neck and say goodnight to Agnes and to Olaf, who has filled the room with cigarette smoke.

I retire to my room, where I type the word 'Leila' into my computer. From the Semitic word for 'night'.

As soon as the sun comes up I am dressed and outside. It hasn't been daylight long enough to take the wet and the cold out of the air. I stomp my boots to keep warm. I was taken aback last night, surprised into silence, so much so that I couldn't bring to mind the questions I needed to ask, but now I have pulled myself together. I didn't even give him the measly bag of her belongings that I brought with me. I don't know now, having met him, whether he would be at all interested in seeing the adverts for her shows, the postcards with her work printed on them, mainly boys and girls in various states of undress. I have also brought photographs. There aren't many of the two of us, since we mainly took digital photos and the only physical copies that I had were in frames. I value them too highly to remove them since I was careless with the electronic versions and let them die along with old computers or put them on USB drives that slipped through the cracks of my material life, as things tend to do. Instead there are photos, taken with Polaroid or cheap disposable cameras, of Leda at art school, at dinner parties, younger than I had ever known her, a future ghost, a prototype of my wife, as unavailable to me in those few years as she had been in her childhood. Was she Leda then? Yes, she must have been, since I had met her friends and that was what they called her. I try not to get hung up on the fact that she changed her name. I persuade myself that she didn't think to mention it since it meant so little. And yet I say it over and over again with every step I take, as if I have accidentally pushed a button in my brain and it has jammed. Leila, Leila, my foot hits the ground, Leila, my leg bends at the knee, Leila, Leila, Leila.

I hope to catch Olaf early, smoking on his front porch or warming the engine of his car. He isn't at home. I hang around and leave a note.

Agnes is making breakfast when I return, still in her nightclothes, and scolds me for being up so early. I nod and make an exaggerated expression to encourage her to mother me. I sit at the table and watch her cook, hoping that she will offer me some of whatever sits in the pan, some sort of red sausage, yellow egg.

'What do you think of Olaf?' I ask.

'He's quiet. I don't know him very well. He drinks too much.'

'Leda never talked about him. Leila.'

'You didn't know your wife had changed her name?' Agnes asks, prodding with a wooden spoon at a solidified lump of egg.

'No. Do you think that's strange?'

'A little. But don't be upset. It's nothing.'

'Maybe you're right.'

I press my lips together. There is a savoury smell that clings to the walls here, from the constant movement of lit gas and protein.

Then it dawns on me. Agnes could translate the letters.

'Would you be able to look at something for me?' I ask. 'Olaf wrote letters to my wife for years but she never opened them. Could you read them and tell me what they say?'

Agnes gives me a strange look.

'I'll look at them.' I imagine that for an instant she considered what she was about to do to be unethical but that curiosity has won her over. I retrieve the letters from my room and Agnes almost snatches the fat envelope from my two hands. She spreads them out on the table and takes her hair up away from her face with an elastic band. Then she sits down to read them.

'They don't say much,' she says, 'they just ask questions. "How are you?" "How is school?"' She pauses and picks up one of the letters, and then another. She studies them closely. 'There are some poems.'

'Oh?' I ask. I have to fight the urge to rip the letters out of her hands, as if by sheer will alone I could understand them.

'I don't recognise them, but there is a line here… I will try and translate it but it is difficult. It is about a girl walking through a city with – flowers in her hair.'

'Do you think Olaf might have written that?'

'Him?' Agnes gives a snort of derision. 'No. He copied it from a book or something.'

'One of the letters had something in it,' I say. I take the lock of hair from my pocket and put it on the table in front of me. 'That's my wife's hair,' I say. Agnes looks at it but doesn't move to pick it up. She screws her face up and says, 'Huh.'

'What do you think it means?'

'How am I supposed to know?' she says. She seems annoyed with me suddenly, and pushes her chair back to return to the breakfast, which has been cooling on the unlit stove. She inspects the meat, pushing it with one finger, her back turned to me.

'Is there anything else in the letters?' I ask.

'This is none of my business,' she says. She doesn't bother turning round. 'Anyway, most of it doesn't make sense to me. That fool speaks Latvian worse than he speaks English. He must have skipped school to hunt boar.'

I ask her to underline the part with the poem. She does so, hardly looking at the page. Before I leave she silently hands me a plate filled with black bread and a spoonful of the chalky egg.

June 1995.

Yesterday I got the highest mark in art class and the teacher gave me a note to take home to Petra. When she opened it she sniffed and looked me up and down. No more playing violin, she said. We can sell the violin because it was very expensive. Then she folded it up and put it in her top pocket as if she were a magician and for the rest of the evening I kept expecting to see the note materialise in different places (for instance under my plate at the dinner table, floating in the bath water, on my pillow). Instead it turned up this morning as I was scraping egg shells into the compost bin. It lay there like a dropped handkerchief. It said I showed great promise and that there were ways of ensuring my future success. The rest of the note was illegible because it had been wrapped around a brown apple core. Abracadabra! I said. What did you say? Petra asked. She was standing right behind me. I said, nothing. Can you take these things over to your uncle's house please? she asked. While you're there you can help Olaf with his homework. He's not doing so well. We can't all be blessed with a giant brain. I said, I don't feel very well. Petra just stood there, staring. You ate three eggs, she said. I had to admit she was right. On the way there I threw up the eggs at the side of the road. I know it's impossible but I swear to God that one of the yolks came up whole.

I can't match the line of poetry with anything on the internet, and start to wonder whether the phrase has been misspelled, or simply misremembered. I don't know much about Latvian poetry. I read a little about it, a few poems I can find that have been translated into English, then I start to feel sleepy. I lie on my back and digest my breakfast. I can feel my body working away to turn it into steps and heartbeats. Meanwhile I stroke the lock of hair. I fall asleep dreaming that a cat is curled up on my stomach, purring.

Agnes tells me Olaf is away a lot, hunting, visiting cronies, doing odd jobs in neighbouring villages. He spends most of his nights at a clubhouse, which she marks for me on the map. She wrinkles her nose when I suggest that she accompany me there, saying that the place is full of 'criminals'.

I go along to attempt to commandeer some of his time, hoping to hold it together long enough to ask him questions. I want to know what his relationship with Leda was, why he wrote to her, why she never acknowledged his letters or his existence. Why, when my friends (so much more open, enquiring than I could ever pretend to be) asked Leda at a late dinner in August (all the doors and windows open to try and encourage a breeze to push its way through the stifled air) about her family back in Latvia, she had shrugged and said that there was nobody left.

The clubhouse is barely more than a converted garage, with a burnt carpet and a bar stocked with preposterously large bottles of vodka and balsam. There are round wooden tables and bar stools and a large television that plays constantly on mute.

When I find Olaf in a dark corner he is aloof and taciturn with me. The first evening he barely acknowledges me and I spend hours having my ear chewed off by one of his friends, none of whom holds any special appeal for me. The second night he assents to me joining in one of their card games as they are a man short. I learn the rules quickly, and because I'm the most sober participant by a long shot, I start to win. The men quickly change games if they think I'm doing too well. This means that within the week I have become accustomed to several card games. I never really know if I am playing well or just by some coincidence not enraging the men that sit around the table. When I win Olaf slaps me on the shoulder and laughs. I feel that I have made progress.

It is basically true that being adept at these games earns these men's respect. They also talk about each other's hunting skills. One of them, named Maris, is apparently mathematically gifted, from what I can gather (most of the men speak Latvian rather than Russian and sometimes forget to translate for me). His virtues are extolled to me while he sits with his hands clasped between his legs in a way that is feminine and awkward. It reminds me of when Leda would fall asleep on the sofa in front of the TV or after staying up late reading. I would find her curled foetally with her hands between her thighs, and I knew that she looked then as she must have looked as a child. This man sits upright, smirking with false humility as the others tell me how quick his mind is, what a magician he is with numbers. I don't trust him. I think he is probably some sort of shyster, but I don't dare contradict the prevailing mood. I rarely say a word, in truth. I look to Olaf for the correct response. If he laughs, I laugh. If he drinks, I drink. I can feel my stomach swelling with the daily bouts of drinking. I don't get drunk quickly but I do feel the effects strongly the next day. I've barely recovered from my nausea and the heavy feeling that lies behind my eyes when I realise that it is the evening again, and time to tread the path to the clubhouse where already massive amounts of beer and wine are being consumed by men who have already done manual labour, bathed and dressed and fed children, done complicated mental arithmetic, and thought correctly about guns. I get there and Olaf surveys me briefly before returning to whatever conversation he has been having.

At the end of another long evening I grab his hand and I say, 'She never mentioned you,' but the room is loud. His friends are chanting and singing. He casts off my hand.

I see a change in his demeanour when a man named Georgs brings in his dog, a mongrel. The dog is part German shepherd and has the eyes of a war criminal. Olaf becomes withdrawn and is even quieter than usual, rarely raising his eyes to join in the conversation around him and drinking his beer in a more focused way, as if he means to get drunk on it.

'What is it?' I ask him. Across the table, Maris's eyes roll and he shakes his head at me. When Olaf has gone to the bathroom he beckons me closer.

He tells me that one of Olaf's neighbours had a dog who kept him up all night barking. Olaf poisoned the dog. Or rather, he mixed some chopped liver with ground glass and fed it to him. The dog ate the glass, suffered massive internal bleeding and died a violent and prolonged death. Ever since, Olaf has been convinced that dogs are out to get him. He suspects that they are conspiring against him and will somehow bring about his demise. This is why when Georgs's dog whines and pulls at its lead, he tenses and the sinews of his neck become pronounced like the roots of a tree breaking the ground.

I can't judge whether Olaf is paranoid or not, as I can't read into the dog's behaviour. Whether he seems unduly hostile or his eyes flash darkly from time to time in Olaf's presence, I can't say. Perhaps the dog is simply tired and hungry and wants to get back home, away from the drunken squalor of the club.

On my way back to the house one evening a car passes and the driver is someone I recognise. I have to stop myself shouting out. Of course it is not the person I think it is. The chances of me bumping into this person in a cafe in Hampstead sitting over a veal schnitzel are remote, but this – this is ridiculous. I realise I have spent five or six days simply drinking and playing cards. Perhaps I am losing touch with reality, spending so much time in the fug of the men's lives here. I haven't heard from the university since I got here and I leave longer intervals between checking my emails. I swap the bag I am carrying, full of tinned fruit that one of the men has for some reason given me as a gift, from my right hand to my left and flex my fingers, which have striped purple and white and are painful. I remember now. I won the tinned fruit playing cards.

I decide to go up to my room through the front entrance of the house. I walk through the door, which as usual swings on its loose hinges and bangs against the side of the building. The kitchen is fogged with cigarette smoke and damp laundry. I put the bag down on the counter. Agnes is sitting at the table with three dark-eyed women, one of her feet up on a chair. She doesn't interrupt her story for my entrance, but the others all turn their attention from her to stare at me. Eventually she trails off and whips her head around.

'You!' she says, accusingly. Then she rolls her eyes and gestures with her cigarette. 'This one walks all day. I've never known such walking. What's to walk for? I give him the bus timetable.'

'You're staying here?' A thin woman with a jutting chin addresses me. I say that I am.

'He was married to Olaf's cousin,' Agnes says.

'Who is Olaf?'

'He's a hunter,' I say. 'He hunts.' They laugh.

'Everybody hunts here,' Agnes says. Then she says something in Latvian to the thin woman, and she nods. 'She knows who Olaf is. Would you like to sit? What have you eaten? This one doesn't eat.'

Agnes lifts her foot from the chair next to her and folds her leg to sit on it. I sit down with a terrible sickness in my throat and stomach. There is a plate of cured ham on the table and a loaf of dark bread and there is also a plastic tub of yellow margarine. I spread some on my bread and the chemical and rancid smell rises in my nose and throat. The bread is rich with caraway. I chew it and imagine growing up with such a taste in my childhood mouth. I think of Leda's mouth chewing on it and imagine idiotically for a second that I had been able to taste it when we kissed. Agnes taps ash onto a small decorative plate on the table. She asks me what I have learned from Olaf. I find myself attempting to string something together but I lose confidence in the sentence and let it trail off. 'It's hard to get him alone,' I say. Agnes sniffs and shakes her head.

This evening the men in the club are dejected, because they haven't killed anything. Their conversation is stilted, and even though I can only understand some of the things that they say, I can tell that their jokes are strained. It feels as if they each blame the other. I feel unhappy too. I uncharacteristically try to cheer them up, buy round after round of drinks that are swallowed wordlessly, and make motions towards the cards that sit untouched on the bar. But nobody feels like playing. Desperately I talk to Olaf. How long had they hunted for? What went wrong? Had they had any sight of the wolves? Though none of these are particularly the questions that I would like to ask. He shakes his head and sighs. He pulls at the ends of his moustache between his index and middle fingers. He leans in and says something I can't make out.

'What?' I ask.

'Georgs,' he says, and then in English, 'Georgs is a bad man.' It seems to take all his strength to muster these words for me, and he sinks back into his chair again.

'Why is Georgs a bad man?' I ask. I ask the question three or four times. Each time Olaf gets increasingly impatient with me. Eventually he tells me with a knotted brow to be quiet. I feel paranoid and sick in this environment, so I shut my mouth and wait until enough time has passed for me to leave without it seeming odd. I needn't have wasted my time. Nobody looks up when I start to put on my coat, except Georgs himself, who seems to be insinuating that I should leave some money behind with which they could pay for even more drinks. I think, Olaf is right. Georgs is a terrible man.

I wander back towards the house, shivering so violently that the muscles around my ribcage and back begin to seize up. This constricts my breathing until I find it difficult to walk. The wind comes in off the Baltic Sea and envelops everything in a salted sheen of ice. It is, inevitably, still light. The days go on and on. Isn't there such a thing as fucking darkness in this place? The forest is silent except for the never-ending dance of the pines, the low moan of their trunks and the crinoline rustle of their needles breaking. I begin to curse Olaf and the rest of the men under my breath. I am drunk and tired. What can I do to find some way back to Leda? I seek for meaning in every miserable glint and shadow, when none of it belongs to me.

In bed I try to summon her again. The weight of her exists, I'm sure of it, on my shoulder, on my stomach there, yes. Wasn't that her hair tickling me below the right temple, that feeling that her face is near enough to kiss? But the air isn't warm enough. The bed holds nothing but me. I gather the blankets around me to try and feel some human bulk that I can recognise as more than myself. I fail. Leila.

★

There is a pounding on the door, the sound of something solid being thrown against something solid again and again. I turn over and pull the covers up over my ears. What time is it? I hear Agnes shouting something in a strangled voice from her bedroom, but she doesn't bother to get up and the sound continues. Eventually I heave myself from the bed and down towards the commotion. My feet slap against the stairs. The cold air infiltrates my billowing pyjama legs and makes my leg hair bristle.

The door is fitted poorly into its frame and at the bottom the night is visible in an inch-thick strip. Or maybe it's only shadow, but still – to put my naked toes so close to it. To have my little piggies stubbed against that black lead. I momentarily consider turning on my heel but I'm so close. I want to prove that the most grown-up, the most responsible, person in the house is me. I put my hand on the curtain and pull it aside to see what terrible monster is out there. It's Olaf. I'm sure he has come to rob me or to find refuge from his horrible life in mine. Suddenly I feel possessive of everything that belongs to me, even my pyjamas. I clutch the shirt closed at the throat.

'Let me in, my friend,' Olaf says. His voice is singsong with booze and I imagine for a hopeless second that we are, after all, in a fairy tale. If I don't invite him inside, if he doesn't guess correctly the

right phrase that might move me aside to let him
enter, he will have to stay outside with the rest of the
animals. Instead he uses the flat of his hand against
my sternum to shove me out of his way and I stand
shivering as he removes his boots. He staggers into
the kitchen, lit by a naked bulb.

'Here, look,' Olaf says, and he throws three lazy
punches into the air. 'I used to be a boxer, did you
know?'

'No,' I say.

'What do you know about boxing?' he says. He
holds his fist just under his jaw, as if waiting for me
to say something that warrants it.

'Nothing,' I say.

'You don't know anything!' Olaf laughs. He lets his
hand fall to his side then looks around the kitchen.
He finds and stuffs his hand into the heel of a loaf
of bread. He puts the soft inside of it in between
his teeth and cheek, like chewing tobacco. In the
bar his face had shown itself in brief glimpses, like
shards of something dull in the ground, but here
underneath the swinging light I can see again how
strangely handsome he is. His presence makes my
nerves stand on end. It's as if I can feel his saliva
softening the bread.

'Let's go and find Georgs,' he says. He smiles.

'It's two o'clock in the morning,' I say. My voice
sounds strange, hysterical.

'I can show you how to punch him.'

'That won't be necessary,' I say. He makes a gargling noise in the back of his throat suddenly, lurches forward and spits something solid into the sink. The sound of Agnes's voice bellows from her room. I can't make out what she's saying but Olaf laughs and makes a dismissive gesture. He thinks we're a team. He thinks that whatever is happening is happening to the two of us. Suddenly being in my pyjamas in the kitchen feels like a bet I have won. I sink against the counter. Olaf pads around in his socks: ribbed, torn and completely black at the soles.

'I know the bitch keeps drink around here somewhere,' he says. I flinch. I remember the wine that I brought. When I presented it Agnes thanked me perfunctorily and stashed it in a cupboard where it sits now among twelve other bottles with their labels variously mildewed. The bottle cost less than a pint of beer back in London and (if she even notices it has gone) I can replace it. I pour us both generous glasses. Olaf is so drunk that at times I struggle to keep track of his slurred mixture of Latvian and Russian.

'Tell me about Leila,' I say, after listening to him drone on in broken sentences about a fight that he lost fifteen years ago. He smiles with an open mouth and I can see a large gap in his teeth where a molar has been removed by force or design.

'No,' he says, carefully, 'you tell *me* about Leila.'

'What do you want to know?'

'She just died, like that? All of a sudden?'

'That's right.'

'She was depressed.'

'No, not really. It wasn't suicide, if that's what you mean.'

'That is not what I mean.' Olaf laughs. 'I mean she was depressed. She talked about dying all the time.'

I can't decide whether this is true. Why can't I decide? She talked about death in an abstract way, as a matter of interest. Did she talk about her own death? Olaf is watching me through wet eyes. 'Oh yes,' he continues, the words lolling on his tongue, 'it was obvious she would die before any of us. Even though it didn't work that time.'

'What time?'

'The time she filled her pockets with stones.'

'Oh no,' I say. 'You're thinking of Virginia Woolf.'

'No, Leila filled them with stones. It was in her diary.'

'I didn't know she kept a diary,' I say. My tongue feels huge and bee-stung in my mouth.

'She left it lying around and my aunt Petra got hold of it. It said she filled her pockets with stones and walked into the sea. It didn't work because the waves washed her straight back onto the beach.'

'Just an adolescent fantasy,' I say, 'surely.'

Olaf shrugs and sips his wine. 'Good that you came here. Good that we have each other now. Why don't we go upstairs and wake up Agnes?'

'Better not.'

'Yes, we're practically brothers. I'll teach you how to play a prank. We'll wake up Agnes now.'

'I don't want to cause trouble.'

'You can cover her mouth and I'll take off her night dress.'

'What are you talking about, Olaf?' I say. I slam the glass down. 'What are you saying to me?'

'I'm joking, calm down.' Olaf pushes the glass across the table and back into my hand. 'But you shouldn't invite men into the house at this time of night.' He wags his finger. 'That's no good. If Georgs had been here it would be a different story altogether.'

We drink for a couple more hours until Olaf makes no sense to me. He tells broken stories about a young Leila, sings songs that sound like threats. We cry a little bit, both convinced of our own sorrows. When I finally open the door I am startled by the deep blackness. The light, grim and resolute here, breaks so completely. I stand swaying at the door as Olaf retreats into the distance. Then, barefoot, I step out. I wander like a sleepwalker with my hands outstretched, flinching as I reach the forest and touch the branches, the horrible stage whisper of cobwebs against my neck. I walk as straight as I can for as far as I am able. Then I stand in a tiny clearing, helpless as a crustacean waiting for the crush of the tide. My feet sink into a patch of moss. The pines creak. I panic, suddenly. I scour the slim grey breaks in the branches. There's a moon somewhere. I breathe the cold air. Eventually, I hear them. The wolves howling. I close my eyes. Fear is in my chest and groin. Perhaps if I close my eyes, I will sleepwalk myself back to the house, and up to bed, or to somewhere else, somewhere that makes sense.

April 1996.
One of Petra's friends got me a job serving coffee at the airport. She's also encouraging my painting. Petra takes what she says very seriously. She says, she's an intellectual and she knows things. This intellectual woman lives in Riga and she lets me stay at her apartment if I have an early shift. I'm spending a lot of time there.

I bought a new shirt with the money. As soon as I had buttoned it up all the way to my chin, I knew that it was the perfect shirt. I went downstairs and stood in the kitchen waiting for my mother to notice me.

'This is what I look like now,' I said.

She said, 'Mm-hmm,' and carried on reading her racist newspaper.

There's just enough room inside the shirt for me. This almost never happens. I'm supposed to wear the same sized shirt as some other woman, a woman who was born in a different year and uses different phrases. She spits in the sink or shrieks in the cinema when something scary happens. She rolls her Rs correctly, she flushes the toilet without looking, she doesn't write a diary, she chews chicken bones, she holds her breath when she walks past the butchers, she frowns at her chipped manicure. She makes people guess what the secret ingredient is in her casserole. She writes poetry, she hates poetry, she has an opinion about poetry, she doesn't ever think about poetry, she has a lazy eye, she has a rich husband, she takes in stray cats, she sings in a choir. She wears the same shirt as me but this time the shirt doesn't fit her very well, it gapes around her breasts or pinches under the armpits or comes untucked from her trousers because this shirt was made for me. I think I would quite like to wear just this shirt and a long black skirt for the rest of my life, that way people will know what to expect from me and I'll have a recognisable visual identity, like Cher.

I look down and see it. A tick, embedded in my leg. God, it has been feasting on me for hours. It is fat and nearly black and hard like a stone, and in fact that's what I mistake it for at first. It is only when I put my shin up onto the thigh of the other leg to get a good look that I see it is a living thing. I prod it experimentally. It is stuck firmly. I decide to shower anyway. The soap foams in the horrendous-smelling water as I lather my genitals, and runs down over the tick. It is disgusting. I have to get it off. You can't just wrench a tick free, I know that much. Perhaps I could burn it – did I remember the image of a man in an overcoat using the hot end of his cigar in this way, or did I merely invent it? I don't have a cigar but I have tobacco and cigarette papers, extremely old and dry at the bottom of my overnight bag. Remnants of an old life, evenings with Leda where we would smoke chubby marijuana cigarettes with her friends and take long walks in the dark across the heath, convinced that we were somehow lost and growing more and more hysterical. How small everything must have seemed to Leda, I realise now – how pedestrian the expanses of grass and patchy woodland, the brambles that snagged our cuffs and the rabbits that darted ahead of us, making us scream. She did such a good job of pretending that everything was wild and magical. But it wasn't.

I dry my hands on the towel and try to roll a cigarette. It is clumsy and grains of reddish tobacco spill from the end of it as I stick it between my lips. Could I drown it, I wonder? I light the cigarette and inhale too harshly so that I almost throw up. I bring the cigarette a millimetre away from it but then I lose faith in the technique completely. I don't dare go near the thing in case I accidentally separate its body away from its head and its horrid little jaws. If that happened I would have to dig out the remains of it with a pair of tweezers. I don't have a pair of tweezers. Perhaps Agnes does. Or I could use nail scissors. I could just as easily find someone who knows what they are doing. Probably ticks feed on the people round here as a matter of course. I dress in loose trousers and a shirt and make my way down the stairs. I walk as if I have a splint on my leg. I've always hated the idea of parasites of any kind. That was one of my many pertinent arguments against pregnancy. I shout 'Agnes?' and the sound of my voice falls upon the walls of the house. She isn't in. That's obvious. Her bike isn't in its place. What time is it? I start to feel panic rising in my blood. So stupid. A little tick, an insect no bigger than the nail of my ring finger. I'm an idiot, a child. I sit on the stairs and take a firm grip on its distended body, and pull slowly. It comes away like a splinter, with its head intact. I find a little coffee cup and put the tick upside down in it, where it looks like a fat little spider. I bring the cup up to my face and peer closely at the thing.

'Fuck you,' I say. It just lies there.

The post is delivered to a group of letterboxes at

the eastern edge of the village, presumably because the various houses and farms are difficult to get to in inclement weather. Their owners check them every so often and other times don't, so that the postman is forced to stuff newspapers and leaflets and letters into the overflowing boxes. I'm heading past them in that general direction with the faint hope of finding a school that I have marked on a map that Agnes gave me. In her opinion it is almost definitely where Leda would have gone to school, and I want them to check their records. I have an idea of seeing her name carved into a bench or a tree, of hearing children play and seeing a doorway through which she would have passed hundreds of times. Being here, looking for these things, is like waiting for a photograph to develop.

The sun is shining and the light seems very clear. A group of wagtails fly from the trees to the ground and back again, their black eyes staring. I bet you'd eat that tick, I think. Wouldn't you? I carry on walking until I come to the road, where the dirt turns into fine gravel, the texture of which my feet recognises wrongly as snow. I haven't much idea of where I am going, only that there doesn't seem to be much of a margin for error. There is just one road and I follow it. I feel completely restored by the successful removal of the tick. I'm surprised to appreciate that the place is beautiful. Everywhere

I look inspires some pastoral reverie that, if I were a different human being, would no doubt express itself artistically. Leda left this place to paint swans on a dirty little boating lake in North London. Why couldn't we have moved here, the two of us, and played cards with her cousins and raised animals that we later killed for great celebratory feasts? She probably saw it differently. Was it really that she liked vegan food and dog shows? What could have been so extraordinarily awful about her connections to her past that she traded them in for the pretence of having none at all? I realise now I'm an intruder of sorts, a time-travelling interloper. Is there something distasteful about me being here, after all? What did I talk about with Olaf last night? But I can't remember.

I walk past two old men carrying a headstone. Occasionally one stops to rest his load on the ground, wipes the sweat from his eyes and leans his weight forward with his hands on his knees. The other stares impassively until it is over. It starts to rain.

After about a mile and a half I come upon a church. I'd noticed it on the way in from Riga, in fact. It is large and angular and unattractive. I can hear that an organ is being played inside. Is it Sunday? I have no idea. I approach it cautiously. The organ is very loud. I try to make out the tune but it changes as soon as I listen. An old woman sits just inside the entrance, next to a donations box. Actually, it is a donations basket. She is on a mobile phone and gestures irritably towards the basket as I reach into my pockets and offer her a couple of coins. She spits into the phone as I pass further into the building, '*Nekad! Nekad!*'

December 1999.
I got back from Paris last night. Tomas met me off the train but I was bored just looking at him. We walked around for a little while in the cold sunshine and I looked at everything through my green sunglasses and made excruciating small talk until I couldn't stand it any more. Eventually I had to say, Tomas, do you see that woman over there? It was the woman who was selling gossip magazines and sandwiches just outside the station. She was wearing earrings shaped like snowmen. It's not even November, I pointed out to Tomas. I think he knew what I meant. He thinks he's a hot shot because he owns a bar in Ventspils, but only poor families go there and they haven't changed the menu since the last owner died. Pork and potatoes. I said by the way I'm a vegetarian now, Tomas. He said oh right and am I getting enough iron, that kind of thing. He could tell I had made significant fortifications to my castle walls and

that his army was no longer strong enough to consider the invasion. I'm reading a self-help book that says every new experience contributes to our emotional architecture. That's why I'm talking about castles etc. It's very useful because I can think of myself as both the princess and the tower. Tomas's allergies were unfortunately affecting him quite badly so we sat in a booth in a dark pub. Every so often he would use the corner of a paper napkin to dab at the fluids leaking from his eyes. I thought, it probably looks like we're breaking up already. So I broke up with him.

I've not had the chance to break up with anyone before. So I made the most of it. I'd been thinking of different ways to devastate him and I made sure to get through them all. At the end I was laughing for some reason. 'I don't think this is about me,' he said, but I interrupted him and said that it definitely was.

Afterwards I bought myself six pastries. 'Are you having friends over?' the baker asked me. I just smiled mysteriously and then when I was outside I sat on the kerb and took off one glove and started to eat them. They were round choux buns with vanilla cream, about the size and shape of apricots. I ate five and then wrapped up the last one and put it in my handbag. A car went past and two teenagers hung out of the windows and leered at me. I saw there was a girl in the back seat and she was looking at me too. I remembered all the reinforcements I'd been making to my emotional architecture. 'Hey!' I said. 'Watch the fucking road!' They called me a psychopath and revved off and I watched the girl's black ponytail get smaller and smaller.

When I got home my mother took the pastry from its wax paper and said, 'What is this? What is this? A time bomb for my behind, that's what.' We sat up late and watched TV and she ate it slowly, making purring noises. Is it nice, I asked. She said it was.

While I am admiring a fresco there is a commotion at the entrance of the church. A woman has arrived and is arguing in English with the old guard at the door. I don't know she is speaking my language at first because she has an accent that renders her speech incomprehensible to me until I recognise it as German. It's funny how that can happen, how we have to tune into an accent like a radio station, and how before we have done so it is unfathomable static.

Curiously, the woman is shouting, in English, 'I can speak Russian, I can speak Latvian, I can speak German.' She is wearing a long black coat and stands in a puddle of water. I ask if I can help and she looks at me spitefully. The old lady points at the basket and I realise that the problem is that she has no money. I look for a few more coins in my pockets and put them in. This satisfies the old woman and she sits back down with a smile on her face. The woman in the black coat eyes me with contempt and walks straight past me into the church, where she arranges herself at the end of a pew. Her coat spills over the side and onto the floor where it continues to weep rainwater. She takes her gloves and carefully wrings them out, wipes a tissue under her eyes to remove the mascara that has collected like pressed moths' legs, and sighs.

I sit down next to her. She says her name is Ursula. She is cold and wet from being taken by surprise by a rainstorm, as fucking usual, she adds. I wonder how, if it is usual, she was taken by surprise by it. Instead I nod. It's true that the clouds collect and disperse above the trees here like smoke curling from a mouth, that the sun can be shining and thunder breaking at the same time. She hitched a ride from a friend part of the way to a nearby seaside town that is renowned for its water sports. The friend would now be on a jet ski, she surmises. She thought she'd walk the last few miles over the course of the day, stopping to rest and read her book. But by the time she got here she was soaked and she had abandoned her book, a sodden brick, by the side of the road. Actually she had hurled it into the forest. She says, it might be fun if somebody found the book several years from now by wandering along a path that happened to intersect with the trajectory of her throw that afternoon. It's a dirty book, she admits. It's badly written but it makes her laugh and once in a while it's actually sexy. She casts her eyes to the ceiling. She doesn't ask God for forgiveness. She simply smiles. Then she pulls up her skirt and says, 'Look at this.' The thing that she wants me to see is a purple graze about the size of my middle finger, behind her left knee. It hurts like hell, she says, and she gets in a terrible mood when she is in pain. 'I just want to lie down and cry,' she says, 'like a baby.'

'How far are you from where you're staying?'

'About another twenty minutes, but I'd rather sit here and wait for the rain to stop. I got this cut from stumbling about a mile back when I tried to take a shortcut. I should have driven but I was feeling energetic. It's so strange to meet an Englishman here, of all places. Are you lost?'

'No,' I say. 'My wife grew up here.'

'Yes, whereabouts? Maybe she can help me. I'm actually looking to build some property nearby but I'm getting nothing but trouble.'

'I'm afraid she's no longer with us.'

'Where has she gone?'

'Oh, she's dead.'

Ursula's eyes widen and she crosses her arms and sits back on the pew. An errant droplet figures its way down her narrow, angular face and sits in the crease between her nose and cheek.

'Why not just say that, then? You've made me look insensitive.'

'I think it's an English thing.'

'Of course it is! What did you say? She's no longer with us? It makes me think, oh she's visiting family or something. Then you say she's dead. I know many different languages and there are always games with them that only native speakers play. The trouble is, the games are usually about the most important things. Sex and death. Always people want to skip past the subject or dress it up so it's unrecognisable. The only English way I know to say that somebody is dead is that they passed away. Couldn't you have said that?'

'I hate that phrase.'

'Oh, me too! It's so peaceful, like putting paper inside an envelope. I won't pass away, that's for sure. I'll make a lot of noise. I'll roll around in my coffin. It will be like a pinball machine, extremely irritating.'

'My wife was killed by a swan.'

'Oh my God. And you choose to say "she's no longer with us"? What are you scared of, that the truth is too interesting?'

'Are you allowed to say that in here?'

'What? My God? He doesn't mind. He's eavesdropping. Move along, God. We're discussing this poor man's wife. Hopefully she is being looked after.' She indicated the ceiling above us with one pointed nail, or rather she indicated the much larger idea that floated above it.

'I don't know.'

'Wasn't she a good person?'

'Yes, she was, but I'm Jewish and I don't think Jews believe in Heaven.'

'What? Don't you know what you believe in?'

'I don't know what I'm *supposed* to believe in.'

'I'm not religious but in here it's best to play it safe. Look at our friend.'

I crane my head over my shoulder to see the old lady sitting with her legs far apart and her hands clasped in front of her. She has fallen asleep and her head lolls so far forward that her chin touches her breastbone and the back of her neck makes a powdered surface so flat you could sit a glass of iced tea on it. I also see through the arch of the open door a perfect domed section of white sky, which sits in the pool of water on the stone steps too.

'It isn't raining any more,' I say. Ursula sighs and slaps one glove on top of the other, as if encouraging a stubborn horse. Then she stands up and grimaces at her wet feet.

'I have to get my feet dry,' she says, 'or I'll get pneumonia. Maybe an old wives' tale or maybe good common sense. I don't want to risk it. That's how you pass away. But if you care to join me we can carry on our conversation and you can help me with my bag.'

'All right,' I say. 'Do you know I had a tick on my leg this morning?'

'What are you telling me that for? I don't want to know.'

Ursula is staying in a wooden cabin on some land that belongs to wealthy friends, both doctors in Riga. The cabin is set up with a double bed, a kitchenette, a desk and a cot, piled with dozens of paperback books and a blanket.

'That's my nook,' Ursula says, fondly. 'I wish I could take it with me when I leave.'

She heats a pan of water on the gas stove and ushers me into one of the folding chairs. She finds her phone and asks me to choose some music while she gets changed behind a large screen that has been fashioned out of a faded pink material embroidered with gold thread that breaks and falls away in large patches. When she rematerialises I am still sitting in the same place, staring at the phone she has given me, not knowing how to find music on it. I say, 'I couldn't decide,' and she says, 'Hmm. Come on. Anything at all. I have the world at my fingertips.'

'Anything will do,' I say, because I'm sick from having listened to Brahms for days but can't think of a single other composer, musician or band. I want to appear relaxed, so I scan the room for something to rest my eyes on in an interested fashion. I gaze out of the window, which is open but covered with mesh to prevent insects from coming in. I've been bitten several times by mosquitoes, and, as usual, the bites have swollen and are a constant irritation under my socks and where the cuff of my trouser leg grazes them. The sky is grey and mottled. Ursula props her phone in a teacup, which acts as a sort of sound amplifier. It is a pretty terrible excuse for a speaker, but I can't help but be faintly charmed by her. She is thin and therefore brittle-looking, but her eyes and jewellery both flash with colour and she expresses herself with broad gestures of her hands. Every movement she makes looks substantial. She pours us wine.

'The tea...' I say, stupidly. I've no idea why I'm so concerned with drinking tea all of a sudden. She glances at me while she fills our glasses with a purple Cabernet and smiles.

'The water is for my hot water bottle,' she says. 'I feel the cold.'

When the water starts to steam, she pours it into a little yellow hot water bottle, which she wraps in a shirt and holds between her legs while we talk. She tells me she had originally travelled around rural Latvia to interview people who had returned to their country following the declaration of independence in the nineties. She grew tired of hearing and writing about violence and went back to Riga to stay with her doctor friends, the ones whose land the cabin sits on. They offered to put her up here and she stayed for several weeks, sorting through her notes to some extent, but mainly, as she puts it, 'being alone'.

'It's so hard to be alone these days,' she says, absent-mindedly running a finger around the rim of her glass. 'It's practically illegal. My family and friends hound me at every opportunity about when exactly I plan to come back. The truth is, I came up with this idea about a resort out of desperation. I couldn't do nothing, I didn't have the money. But I couldn't stand the idea of my old life any more. Well, you understand.' She wasn't asking me but telling me.

'Actually, I'm starting to miss it.'

Ursula looks sceptically at me and says nothing. She smells sharp; there is a citronella-scented tub of beeswax on the table which she dips into absent-mindedly and rubs into her heels and wrists. I imagine it's to keep the insects away, although she seems quite protected in here. Whatever the reason, the smell is eliciting some Proustian stirrings that I can't quite place; a poisoned madeleine. As I drink the wine I lift the glass so that it fully encloses my muzzle and I inhale the tannic air deeply. God, I hope she doesn't think that I'm trying to look like I'm appreciating the nose on the cheap wine.

I want to tell her that I know the wine is shit, so she thinks me knowledgeable, while at the same time not mention it at all, because I don't want to be rude. Instead I just stare into its depths and she hums along absent-mindedly to the music, which I don't recognise.

'So, I decided to build a resort here. An eco-friendly place remote enough to attract people who are running away from something. Artists, of course. But wealthy alcoholics too. Mostly Riga attracts stag parties. The rest of the country is relatively untouched by foreign tourism. I know people who will help me build the place in return for free bed and board. The trouble is finding the right land. I like it here, but the locals aren't interested in attracting visitors. The majority of the people here consider themselves not Latvian but Livonian. It's an identity distinct to the coast and they want to preserve it.'

'That's hardly surprising,' I say.

'Well, of course. The government tries to encourage only Livonians to settle on the coast and they're making it hard for me to obtain the correct permissions. What do you think? Do you think I'm doing the wrong thing?'

I have no idea whether or not Ursula's plan to bring tourism into the area is objectionable, having not thought about it and not having any opinions either way on the subject. I defer by saying that it is 'admirable but contentious'. I think how well I'm doing in not saying anything of any consequence at all, and therefore risking absolutely nothing, in the company of this person who for some reason I am slightly afraid of. She sighs pointedly and puts her glass down. I wonder whether she is about to ask me to leave, having realised that she made a grave error in inviting me here in the first instance, and is now deeply regretting having done so, since she can't seem to elicit any conversation from me. I flail around madly for a topic I can bring up that I might safely express an angle on whilst also avoiding being provocative. Fortunately Ursula seems to have changed her mind about tossing me back into the forest. I'm not ready to talk to her about my wife, or even Olaf, so I tell her about Agnes.

'Are you fucking her?' she asks, fondling the artful mess at the top of her head. She appears to be fishing in it for an errant object. I watch her fingers prod and massage the knot of hair with fascination.

'No,' I say, slowly, so as not to cause suspicion, even though there's nothing to be suspicious about.

'How disappointing!'

'Well, she does flirt a little,' I say, panicking.

'That's more like it! What do you do? You don't flirt back?' Her hand falls to her lap.

'Of course not. She's just lonely.'

'Don't be so modest. She's bound to be mad about

you. She's probably writing a million sexy poems about you.'

'I don't think she's writing poetry.'

Ursula rolls her eyes. Since she has lit up visibly I try and think of something equally titillating to follow up with. I've been celibate for months. I can only bring to mind the day before I left England, at the barber's. The new assistant who called himself Moose used a large, soft brush to rid my face of the errant hairs that were sticking to it and I accidentally got an erection. I decide not to bring this up.

Ursula stares at me unreservedly. Her eyes are very large and there is a glassy quality about the blue of the irises that is disquieting. I think that almost definitely I am going to kiss her. Despite knowing that, I can see the endless amount of time that stands between this actual moment and the imagined moment of the kiss, and how much energy will be required to cross this particular ravine, and I feel prematurely exhausted. The pathetic truth is that since Leda's death, the scant occasions that I have masturbated successfully have been with the help of pornography. It's not something I've previously had to rely on, but when I try and imagine the sexual act unaided I am prone to conjuring up images of Leda herself, and the act of grieving overpowers me. I decide to keep this to myself too.

After we've made small talk for around an hour

and almost finished the bottle of wine, a large thunderbolt strikes the cabin, as far as I can tell.

'Oh my God,' I say. Ursula stands up and goes outside. When she comes back I notice that she's still holding her wine glass and that she hasn't got any shoes on. I think to myself that this woman is extremely brave.

'What happened?' I ask.

'Come and see,' she says. I stand and follow her out and then around the side of the cabin. She points a finger at the ground and says, 'Look,' and I do. Underneath the window is slumped some sort of a bird. It's blue, or rather the moon makes it look that way. I get a little closer and it becomes obvious that the dead thing is a swan.

'It must have flown into the window and broken its neck,' Ursula says.

'Jesus Christ,' I say. That's all I can say, standing there. I have my socks and shoes on and I'm not carrying my wine glass but I'm still not prepared to see this.

For the ancient Greeks and for Hindus the swan is thought to be able to carry reborn souls, because it exists between the two planes of air and water. But swans are beautiful and it is easy to assign meaning to a beautiful thing. It is also comforting to find significance in chaos. I find meaning in iconography.

I can understand the swan as I stand over it as a symbol of something else. I interpret it in the same way I would if it were framed and hung on a wall. As it lies beneath me, crumpled, I am unable to think of the swan as a seducer or a rapist; instead, it is something else. It is fragile and solid, vulnerable yet able to withstand completely the load-bearing weight symbolising loss. A dropped handkerchief waiting to be retrieved. A surrender. A fault. I see it as a thing half in this world and half in another. Yet if souls do exist in liminal spaces then I prefer to think of them in hotel bathrooms or at the bottom of a freezer in a petrol station, in the soft, wet cardboard around yellow ice cream.

This is too romantic for me. I refuse it. Instead I put my hands on the body of the swan and feel it warm and heavy with too much blood.

'What shall we do with it?' Ursula asks. I say I'm not sure.

What does the Universe want me to do? I keep asking myself this same question. We debate bringing it inside or burying it. In the end we decide not to do those things, but instead to take it deep into the forest and leave it there for the wolves to eat.

I carry the swan with its neck tucked behind its back like a lock of loose hair. Ursula carries her glass of wine. In the other hand she has a powerful torch that she sweeps in front of us as if it is a machete that will cut down bad spirits intent on blocking our path. We walk in silence. Every once in a while we stop to consider our position. I ask Ursula, 'Are you sure this is deep enough?' and she gets unnerved by my question, meaning that we have to go deeper.

I'm carrying the swan in my arms. It smells good. It smells like a pillow that has been slept on by somebody I love. I think that I could carry the swan for the rest of my life, but eventually Ursula has had enough, and she makes me lay it down. She leans forward and strokes it, and then we turn back to the cabin.

I feel as if I am leaving a terrible weight behind, a weight that belonged to me and that I deserved to carry with me, not just tonight, but for ever.

June 2001.

Petra picked me up from the airport, or rather she got a lift with her friend and stood nervously in the arrivals hall with her handbag held in front of her in both hands, daring someone to rob her so that she could scream. When I arrived she gave me a hard hug and then looked at me. You're thin, she said. I explained that I've been very depressed. Lucky you, she said. Now everyone can finally see those cheekbones that I gave you with God's help.

When we got home the good crockery was on the table and there was a new loaf of bread standing in the middle, covered with a pale blue cloth.

Petra said, I thought we'd have a big dinner to celebrate. I stared at the chairs around the table, upright and brown like miserable, sunburned guests. The table was laid for eight people. I did some maths in my head and then the bottoms of my feet and the top of my head went cold. I felt as if I was sinking. I said, who's coming to dinner? Petra met my gaze and gave a thin smile. Everybody, she said. We're all just so proud of you and want to hear all about your new life. I said, Petra, why are you punishing me? I said, please, Petra. She said, why don't you go and get changed? Do you need a nap? Are you tired from your journey? Then she said, wait there, Daughter. I stood in the room, which was empty except for me and a fly. The fly flew in strange right angles, as if negotiating an invisible maze. I felt the vibrations of its wings inside my skull, against the soft, wet mulch in the shape of my brain. I felt the vibrations in my teeth, and they struck against each other. The fly collided with invisible corners and ricocheted away. And then it came close to me. It landed on my forearm. It was unbearably ticklish but I just stood there with the blood pumping through my jaw.

When Petra came back down she had something for me. It was a silver hairbrush, wrapped in brittle newspaper that flaked away in my hands. She said, this has been passed down through generations and now it's yours.

The bristles were yellow. It was tarnished. It was very heavy. It was too heavy. It was the weight of so many dead women and their heavy heads and their handfuls of thick, shiny hair. I looked at Petra and thought suddenly, why doesn't she cut her hair? It lies on top of her head in a chignon, which has simply got fatter with age. She doesn't take herself seriously enough to get a haircut. She thinks that taking yourself seriously is a sin. I cut my hair into a blunt bob when I got to London. That's how she knows that I don't belong to her any more. Petra, I said. Please phone my uncle and tell them that I'm not feeling well and that they shouldn't come for dinner. I'd rather just eat with you. They'll be very disappointed, Petra said. Well, I replied. Let them be disappointed. I only want women at my table tonight.

The first time I met Leda she was in her late twenties but there was something about her that made me think she was older. In fact I had embarrassed myself by guessing her age and getting it wrong. We were standing in a gallery looking at some work that she had produced. Her friend Amber was there, being thin next to us. Amber didn't think much of me and she goaded me into saying the thing, which was a number. The embarrassing number was thirty-four.

'How flattering,' Leda said. She was smiling at Amber. Amber was smiling at me.

'This beautiful girl? This child? This—' I forget what else Amber said. I excused myself and went to the bathroom, where I sat with my head in my hands on the very edge of the toilet seat. I'd just been dumped by an English girl and was feeling very low. Nobody at work thought very much of me. I thought that the students would flirt with me but actually they ignored me and frotted against each other while I was trying to speak. Amber was a Fine Art PhD candidate and everybody found her very exciting because she was horrible. The most interesting thing about Amber was that she took herself very seriously and was well respected but it turned out that she also ran a psychic hotline. When I reappeared, Leda was at the bar persuading a frightened young waiter to give her free champagne. I thought it would impress her if I bought a bottle, but instead she was disgusted.

'I'm an artist,' she said. 'I shouldn't ever have to buy alcohol.'

'But I bought it,' I pointed out.

'You don't get it,' she said, sneering. Eventually the waiter filled her glass. It was grubby from her fingerprints.

'Do you have work in the show?' I asked. She took me to a corner of the room and showed me a piece I'd seen earlier, a pencil study of a young girl standing at a window. It was so ordinary that I didn't know what to say. And yet because she had done it, it took on new life for me. I saw a very straight L in the corner of the page and instead I asked her what it stood for.

'Leda,' she said.

'Oh, really?' I asked. 'Well, it's a lovely piece.'

'I know,' she said, smiling and gripping the bulb of her champagne glass with her whole hand. 'It's boring. But that's what these old men are into. I learned that the hard way. I sell so many postcards of these pretty girls. And portraits of their animals. English people love their pets. Dogs. Parrots. Business is booming.' She winked at me. She had lowered her voice, I noticed.

'What about personal expression?' I asked her.

'I have rent to pay, so.'

I couldn't place her accent, in part because it was so slight. I filled her champagne glass with the bottle that I was cradling like a baby and after we'd finished it she asked me if I wanted to go back to hers. In the taxi I was trying not to smell her hair as she leaned her head on my shoulder. She didn't look up at me as she said, 'I'm too lonely to have sex with you,' and I laughed because I thought she was making a strange joke. Her sheets were very white and her mattress very hard. It refused the weight of my body even as she added to it by climbing all over me as if she were some excited child conquering a hill and shouting that she was queen. We kissed for a while, but mainly she pinched me. She took fleshy bits of me between her thumb and forefinger while she was talking and squeezed.

I left while she was still sleeping. I thought that I had fucked up, that she would be offended, but I hadn't; she wasn't. I called the following weekend and she invited me for tea. I walked quickly along her road with my heart in my mouth. At her door I had to stop and catch my breath. She made me hold a mirror in front of her while she trimmed her fringe. The steam from the tea smelled sweet, of liquorice.

'This is a bit bohemian for me,' I said.

'You're so English,' she said, with pins in her mouth.

'That reminds me,' I said, 'where are you from?'

There was a game that Leda and I would play when we were tired and wanted to be romantic: we'd swap ideas of what loveliness was. For example: I love the way your jaw cracks when it shuts; I love the unfinished things you say in your sleep like How About We and Can I Please; I love the squareness of your palms; I love the way gold smells when you've been wearing it; I love to hear you talk on the telephone while you are making food and impatient to eat it; I love how aggrieved you feel with your own sickness; I love your equine body slowly fading in the bathroom mirror when you are showering and when it is finally gone and there is a square of grey fog I listen to the hiss of the water and I look down at my own body squat from perspective and from booze and lack of movement I admit and I wonder whether I deserve to be standing here. The last one was mine.

I play the game alone, silently, while Ursula undresses and lies beside me and it goes: I love your body; I love that you can't see mine because you are lying on top of it; I love the sound of pins pushing into cardboard, which is really the sound of the insects trying to come in through the screen and make meals of us; I love the way memories are made; I love my wife. Where is my wife?

Because it was sudden, because she didn't die on a bed in front of me, in stages, because I couldn't hold her hand and watch her eyes close, there is a part of me that thinks that Leda just disappeared. It is like a magic trick that I refuse to believe, but, like a child, am startled by. I walk slowly around the table, I lift up the tablecloth, I pass my hand slowly over the top hat. I'm blinking in the stage lights, and the audience are laughing, and I smile carefully too, to show that I'm just like them, I'm a grown-up, I'm in on the joke. But the truth is I don't know what happened. I've been left behind. When did the trick begin? When she walked out of the house for the last time that morning? Something tells me it started sooner than that.

I talk to Ursular about Leda and she lies there, listening, breathing through her nose. Then we try to make love but, of course, it doesn't work.

It is nearly light. I don't know what time it is. As I let myself into the house I can hear a wailing from the floor above. When I reach the top of the stairs I can see that the bathroom door is open and Agnes is lying in a bath full of water, crying. I run to her, afraid that she has fallen or hurt herself. The water is grey and has long since gone cold. She claws at my neck and thrashes and soon I am as wet as she is and am practically sitting in the bath with her. I start to laugh. She beats against my back with her fists so that my laughter hiccups but it doesn't stop.

'Why are you laughing? Why do you laugh?'

'Why are you crying? Why do you cry?'

She says that she is lonely. Aren't we all, I say. I pull the plug so the water goes down the drain with mournful burps. The slowness of the moment amplifies her nakedness. Whereas moments before I had approached her as sexlessly as I would a crying baby, suddenly the colour of her nipples is alarming. I feel agony in my heart trying to recall the rosewater of Leda's nipples, but also the black tea, the calfskin, the overripe apricot–coloured nipples of all the

other women I have seen this naked, this close. She
needs my help to climb from the tub. There is a
moment where her mouth angles itself towards
mine and I use my hand to guide her head instead
into the crook of my neck. Her breath billows into
the collar of my shirt, sour with wine.

'Where have you been?' she asks. 'I've been in the
bath for hours waiting for you.' Her lips and eyes
are swollen from crying and she slumps forward.
Her breasts sit on either side of her navel. She looks
miserable and as emaciated as Goya's witches. I sit
her on the edge of the tub and find a thin pink towel
to drape around her shoulders. It is bleached all over
so that it looks like it contains a solar system. 'Where
have you been?' she repeats, her hands making fists
on her knees. I say I met a woman named Ursula.
'Who?' Agnes cries. 'That German?'

'It's time to go to bed,' I say, 'it's very late.' She
stays where she is for a moment. Then she lifts her
backside from the bath. Her flesh parting from the
enamel makes a celebratory noise. As soon as she is
upright the towel slides from her body and makes
a pool around her feet. Then she walks, naked and
with dignity, to her bedroom, and locks herself in.

In my room is a note that Agnes has left for me.

'Olaf came to see you. He is going hunting. Ready
at 6 a.m.'

August 2001.
He was big for his age and round-headed and he had a
gang of little boys that followed him round. He started to
tell the other kids that I let him do things to me. He wasn't
ashamed of it in the slightest. He started to pull my skirt
up in front of the other boys. He told them that I stank,
that I wet my knickers. He told them that I did things
that he had made up names for, and the boys pretended to
know what they were and were disgusted. The boys told
the girls. They started to avoid me. I was glad. But Olaf
followed me home. He sang my name. He brought his
friends. As we got older they took it in turns to try and
kiss me and then did exaggerated impressions of vomiting
and gagging. Actually they did kiss me. I thought that one
of them was very handsome. He pinned me against a tree
and pressed his tongue against mine. Then he grabbed a
pile of leaves and stuffed them into his mouth as if trying
to take the taste away. I carried on leaning against the tree
and watched him spit out the brown mulch. The other boys
laughed and chanted my name the way Olaf had taught
them. Leila, Leila, Leila. I thought I had been kissed. I
was proud of myself. Because I didn't have any friends, I
went home and told Petra. She seemed relieved. Every so
often I still hallucinate that wet leaf smell.

I pull my boots over my feet and stand shirtless at
the window. I've stopped bothering to close the

curtains. I know that in the mornings the cold light will wake me. It creeps over me like fear. It's true that there's a singular reason to be afraid this morning. Since I didn't have time to come up with a good reason not to go hunting with Olaf and his band, I know they'll be approaching the house at any minute to drag me into the forest with guns and the dog. I've barely slept. My stomach feels like it's ready to devour itself, a trap in my guts that strains icily. I bend forward slightly to accommodate it. My forehead leans against the glass. I let out a little moan and my wet breath streaks across it. From downstairs I can hear Agnes playing on her chord organ. At least I will be able to leave without confronting her about the events last night. Then there is a knocking at the door. Surely I'm too ill to go? I've passed social anxiety off as stomach flu before now. It's easy to do since it has so many of the same symptoms. Olaf calls my name.

'Se-eb.'

His voice is like a bear trapped in a sewer pipe. Theatrical. Resonant. Unreasonable. There must be more space inside his chest than in mine. What would it be like to have a voice like that?

We tramp silently into the forest, which thickens rapidly. There are various ravines to cross and the floor underfoot is often disconcertingly soft. At times I see piles of shit that I surmise must be from dinosaurs. The pines dagger upwards like a sprung trap. The mosquitoes whine around my head and land on my neck where I slap them and they turn into brown smudges that spatter my palms. Beautiful bright blue dung beetles are planted like treasures in the dark moss and I lean forward to get a good look at them. Georgs turns round to see me in this position, with my nose inches from the thing, and whistles quickly between his teeth to show disapproval, I think. Either way I stand up straight and follow him and stop letting my curiosity get the better of me. I feel like a ten-year-old boy. Georgs himself treads so surefootedly that it is as if the earth rises up to meet his feet. He belongs in the forest. When I stumble he grins. He is so thin that he can slip behind young pines, his knees buckling like branches.

I trail behind so that Olaf can't see me, because I'm ashamed of something I haven't done yet. I imagine he must be disgusted by my footwear, by the way I'm carrying my gun, by the way the mosquitoes seem to bother me more than they do everybody else. The dog comes back for me when I fall too far behind and sniffs at my legs and crotch. He looks up at me and whines and bothers my feet. I don't trust the dog.

'Leila was always more at home in nature than me,' I say to Olaf, flinching slightly at how easily I use what I have come to think of as her dead name in order to accommodate him.

'When Leila was a girl she would come here to hide,' Olaf says. As he walks his feet make deep red trenches in the brown mud, as if he is lifting fresh skin from the wound of the world.

'Yes, of course,' I say, 'of course,' and then I say it again.

'When my mother and her mother talked about the soldiers who lived in the forest we would listen closely. I think Leila was too young to understand. But she hid, like them. We would walk all through the forest and shout *bang bang coming ready or not*. We threatened to catch her. The sound of her voice gave her away. When we caught her we didn't do anything special. We just shook her. She was not really afraid. It is just a game that children play.'

I think about Leda and her childish voice. I imagine it lifting like a startled bird up from the floor into the branches of the trees and hanging there for a moment. I imagine it is still hanging there now, caught in the needles of the pines.

'Tell me more,' I say, 'I'd love to learn more about her life here. You see I don't know much.'

'That's true,' Olaf replies. 'In fact you know nothing.'

'Well,' I start to protest but of course he is right.

'No more talk. We have to stay quiet now. You'll scare everything away.'

I'm not sure what we're looking for and so I simply walk when the others walk and stop when they stop. They take a long time to light cigarettes and say things to each other in muffled monosyllables and I stand off to one side picking my teeth with the jagged corner of my thumbnail. I'm having stomach troubles. Every so often it mewls and I stop briefly to accommodate the contraction. If Georgs looks back at me I just point at a patch of ground and hope that he presumes I'm enamoured by it. Truthfully I'm semi-convinced that I'm going to have to shit in the forest, which fills me with dread. When I went camping, other boys would climb trees and shit off the branches. I was too tense to even let go fully in the WC knowing that there were boys sleeping on the other side of the wall, let alone expose myself in the woods out of fear that something would crawl up my colon and die there. With every cramp I'm more convinced that something unseemly is going to happen. I stand on one patch of moss and it engulfs my leg completely, up to the knee. I scream pitifully. Georgs looks round.

'Oh, fuck off, Georgs,' I say, under my breath. He just stands there. The dog returns and worries at my knee. I pull the leg loose and continue on with fear creeping up the side of my neck and hooking round my ears like cold spectacles. My shoulder aches from carrying the gun. I don't want us to find a beast here, to kill it. I don't want the inevitable to happen. I pray that we are too loud, too clumsy, but in truth the forest is so robust that it swallows us. Our steps don't interrupt the swathes of root and foliage. The branches we break are dead already, dropped like cigarette ash from up high. The place reaches round behind us and closes in a damp embrace.

I remember the time Leda and I and her two recently married friends visited a place that was very special and important to them, and that involved trekking and scrambling and even rowing at one point. I had sulked because my boots had blackened the ends of my socks and I couldn't get them clean again, even after I had made her red-haired friend climb drunkenly down from the bunk bed in the guest house and scour the laundry room, which was full of spiders and earwigs, for bleach. The reason I couldn't go to the laundry room was because I had no shoes or socks on, and Leda refused to go because she was annoyed that I hadn't entered into the spirit of things, and so it had fallen upon her red-headed friend, Alison, who was kind and also sort of a wild soul (and whom I suspected Leda of having had an earlier lesbian affair with during college, because of the sorts of in-jokes they would make, especially while drunk), to go and find me the cleaning fluids amid the cobwebs and collected detritus of the old house. My socks were from Brora, and cost £50, and Leda admonished me for wearing £50 socks on what she referred to as an 'adventure', though it had been falsely sold to me, before we departed, as a 'holiday'. If she could see me now, in my cashmere shooting socks in fawn marl. Appropriately dressed at last.

I swing the gun over my other shoulder. I think the right one is bruised. I catch up with the others, who have paused, I assumed, to smoke, but who seem now to be conferring. I ask what's going on. Olaf shushes me. It becomes apparent that they have spotted some movement further ahead. They start to spread out, slowly at first, and then disperse as if having agreed their positions beforehand. But without having been informed of the correct place to go, I'm ignorant of their plans. I cast widely around looking for a nod or a point of the finger from Olaf. I am literally following him into battle. Except, of course, our enemy is completely ill equipped, outnumbered, and unaware that we are coming for it. I catch Georgs's eye and he surreptitiously smiles at me, in that sneering way that has made me so suspicious of him all along, and I know he means to get me lost, or worse, killed by a stray bullet from one of these bloodthirsty men's guns. I trail Olaf, naturally. I don't want to kill the beast, whatever it is, but I also can't help beginning to get excited at the prospect of it, dead, heaped on the ground in front of the house, and perhaps someone (who?) asking in hushed tones how we managed to capture it. I would smile and look from Georgs to Olaf and we would just relax our eyes and gesture impossibly upwards, to say that we used our wiles, yes, but that ultimately it had been gifted to us by a greater power. That the universe had willed it to us. It could be a deer, stately, ripe with purpled meat quivering in its flanks. Or a wild boar, with flesh that will need the stink marinated out of it.

The sky is barely visible through the trees. Olaf raises his gun. My stomach crumples, then, like a paper bag, inside me. I dart away, stumbling into a slight ravine covered with wet ferns, and then, hoisting my weight to one side and yanking the loop of my belt desperately, I pull my trousers round my ankles. As I squat there, I hear the sound of a gun going off nearby. There is a flurry of noise, the weight of something tearing through the undergrowth and of boughs collapsing. Olaf shouts once, and then it is quiet except for the steady breeze that whistles constantly through the tops of the trees.

When I reappear, he tells me that they lost it. I ask what it is, and he looks at me coldly. He looks away to some distant place and says that it was a black wolf.

'A black wolf?' I repeat, stupidly.

'Ye-es,' he says, still narrowing his eyes towards the darkness of the forest. 'But we lost it.'

'You missed it?'

'I shot it. But it's gone.'

I'm wild with shame to have missed the event, and something else stirs in me too. I feel an urge to move forward, to grab the thing between my hands and claim it.

'Are we going to track it?'

'We should look for blood. Georgs is ahead.'

I nod. 'I'm sorry I missed it—'

'You were shitting.'

'Yes,' I say. 'Unfortunately I was shitting.'

Georgs and Olaf agree to move in ever-increasing circles to try and find the wolf, which Olaf thinks is perhaps lying dead somewhere. I imagine it as a massive thing that has simply swallowed the bullet into its flesh and continued on. Georgs spots blood smeared on the side of an ivy-choked trunk. We all stand around it, admiring it as it glints darkly, like molasses, and nodding our heads. Olaf slowly walks in a zigzag, from one corner of my vision to the next, deliberately. Georgs goes on ahead, with the dog trailing behind him wagging his tail submissively. I know how he feels.

I wander off for a few paces and then turn to find a visual marker so that I don't get lost. Unfortunately, there is no visual marker. The only thing that isn't part of the forest floor is Olaf himself, who disappears seemingly all at once. There is one fern that is slightly wider than the rest, with a carpet of clover beside it. But as soon as I've committed it to memory, it seems to change. There is what looks like a hole in the trunk of a tree, but as I get further away it appears to be more like a shadow, and there are shadows everywhere. I can't help but think that the black wolf is a fantasy. It really stands for the idea of an animal.

I count my steps away from the wide fern and the carpet of clover and the hole in the tree. I take seventeen steps and then pause, straightening up and shifting the gun again on my shoulder, eventually taking it off and laying it on the ground. I used to count my steps as a teenager. I got into a superstitious way of thinking. That's something I never told Leda, and yet for some reason I was convinced that she knew. When we moved into the house on Ebeth Street we looked the place over and as we stood in the kitchen looking out onto the scrappy front bit of garden, she said, 'Well, it's an odd number.' That's all she said, quietly, clasping her hands behind her. I asked her what that was supposed to mean, and she just raised her eyebrows and said nothing. It's true

I'd never live in an even-numbered house.

I don't believe in bad luck any more, but certain habits stick, and you can't think yourself free of them.

I can no longer see the men but I hear one of them shout Olaf's name, and I hurry in the direction of the sound, stumbling over the uneven ground and feeling my heart thud against my chest. My breaths come painfully and I'm afraid of what I'll find when I get to them, but when I do they just mournfully shake their heads and tell me that the black wolf, if it existed at all, is gone. Georgs says he saw it running upwards into a part of the forest that they can't get to, or don't want to, or are forbidden from entering, it's unclear to me. I'm so relieved that it has escaped us, and I hope desperately that its wound will heal, and that it will stay in the other part of the forest. But what would it have been like to stand over the dead black wolf? Olaf spits on his hand and uses it to clean something from his gun, and then he says, 'Let's go,' and we make our way back to the car.

I volunteer to drive us home, to be helpful. About halfway down the grey road, something comes out of the forest in front of the car, which I am driving at some speed out of pure nervous adrenalin, and there's a horrifying collision. I feel the finality of it as we lurch forward, the belts snapping at our chests as I press the brake down hard. We sit in the dark car for a moment, all of us breathing heavily and the dog straining at his lead and whining, his claws clicking against the window.

I open the door and step out. An alarm chimes incessantly. Heaped at the side of the road is a boar, huge and grey and furred, with a snout that leaks blood so red that for a moment I think that it is a dreadful prank, a horrible parody of an event that could not possibly have happened to me. I bend over it and look at its face. It looks more like a dog than a pig, lying there, its eyes closed and its jaws parted, grinning, so that I can see its yellow tusks and a bright pink tongue like a handful of modelling clay. I put my hand to its side and its fur is coarse and it is warm under my hand and it doesn't move and it is completely dead.

The other men get out and wordlessly take two of its legs each and carry it to the car. They heave it on top of the car, which has a significant dent in the middle of the bumper but is otherwise unscathed. They lash it down and then they climb back into the car and I follow.

I start the car. We sit for a moment then, underneath the thing, our breathing quick and loud, with the engine running. I look at Olaf and he smiles broadly and claps his hand to my shoulder. He turns to Georgs in the back seat, laughing disbelievingly, and says with a grin that we can pretend to have shot it.

He isn't sure if he's made himself clear to me, so he makes eye contact with me and raises his eyebrows and makes a gun out of his fingers and pretends to shoot me with it. 'Bang bang bang,' he says, smiling and cocking his thumb three times. 'A natural-born killer.' I laugh hollowly and drive, slowly this time, back to the village, with the feeling that the car is heavier somehow and more difficult to drive, although I know that it isn't.

Agnes stands over us while we prepare the boar at the back of the house. Bringing home something that I have 'killed' has lifted her spirits. She's flirting with me, which is preferable to her hostility. She buys the story that Olaf and Georgs tell: that I took to the hunt like a duck to water and that the animal we drag off the roof of the car is somehow dead due to my skill and guile. The other men have left and Agnes pours us endless cups of black balsam, which she refuses to touch. I sip at it. I'm grateful that she's in a good mood. I also wouldn't mind being drunk to ease myself into the process of butchering the thing.

Olaf tells me that bleeding the carcass is very important in order to avoid the possibility of sour meat. He ties the body by its remarkably dainty back feet to a hook that has been screwed into a tree, and digs a hole underneath. Agnes puts down a plastic basin to collect the blood that comes at a great pace from a hole made in its jugular. We stand around it drinking the cups of black balsam until the flow of blood slows to an occasional driblet. The stink that it gives off reaches me in occasional gusts, sticking ripely to the back of my throat. I force myself to swallow the dead smell, thinking of Leda and whether she found this normal, whether she took part in the hunts or carried away the plastic basin full of blood as Agnes is doing now. It slops over the rim and onto her hand and down the front of her dress as she walks back to the house with it. Georgs's dog worries at her ankles and she shoos it off, hooking the back door open with her foot and slamming it behind her. The dog whines and sniffs at the bottom of the door, and then trots back to lie meekly beneath the hung boar.

Olaf unravels a hose and aims the jet of water at the beast's belly and back. The pit underneath it fills with pink scummy water and the dog takes tentative laps at it before retreating to sit by Georgs, who is smoking and looking at his phone. I go and stand next to them and he looks up at me. He brings the cigarette to his lips. He is quite handsome, in a rough-hewn sort of way. He stares at me from under his heavy brow as if he can see the patterns of my thoughts and finds them objectionable.

'It stinks?' he asks me. I nod. Yes, it does stink, I

confirm. I can smell it no matter which way I stand. He laughs. Olaf turns round. I shrug and cast my hands around wildly to signify that I don't know what he's laughing at and that I'm not actually laughing. The last thing I want is for Olaf to think that we're conspiring against him. I really don't know how I'll ever get him alone. Georgs pokes his finger into my side, just underneath my ribcage where it is tender, and I recoil sideways like a flamenco dancer. He keeps prodding to punctuate his sentence, which is, 'Seb. Thinks. The Pig. Stinks.' I swat Georgs's hand away. Olaf shakes his head.

'It smells good,' he says. And then he barks, which is what he does instead of laughing. It is a vividly canine expression. Georgs's dog's ears prick up at the sound. He looks over his shoulder again and asks Georgs to turn the hose off, which he does. Olaf throws the hose to the ground and dries his hands on the arse of his jeans. He then comes to sit next to me. It is Georgs who is to skin the boar. He has a small, very sharp thin-bladed knife, with which he cuts around all four legs. Then he cuts perpendicular to the two back legs and down the front of the belly, flicking the skin away from the pearlescent sheen of white fat and tugging it downwards so that it comes away. Underneath the transparent fat show the purple cords of muscular tissue. Olaf leans towards me and says, 'He must be careful around the anus. It's easy to rip the anus and into the intestines. It is very smelly. You can still eat the meat,' he says, nodding reassuringly, 'but it tastes, hmm—'

'Terrible.'

'No, not terrible but very—'

'Gamey.'

'What? Gamey.' He repeats the word aggressively but I can't think precisely of how to explain what it means.

'Strong?' I suggest.

'Yes, strong. Some people don't like the taste. You see he will make little cuts, very delicate cuts. Otherwise he will pop the balloon and there will be shit everywhere.'

'An acquired taste.'

'I don't understand. Pass me the hose please.'

I pass the hose, which is still dribbling water. He aims it towards his shoe, which is caked in mud and blood. Then he rubs his shoe on the grass until it's clean. The process of skinning is lengthy, and Georgs works with great intensity, his cigarette hanging damply from his pursed lips. Occasionally he takes a puff and the smoke billows in front of his face, sheathing it in a grey cloud. Georgs narrows his eyes as they come into contact with the smoke and tear up momentarily. I put my hands between my thighs to warm them.

'Did Leila like to hunt?' I ask. As I say it, a curious thing occurs to me. I realise that I'm starting to think of Leda as Leila. Not all of the time, but now and again. It is as if I had started writing a poem and halfway through become distracted. The poem had been about one person but is now about another person. Or rather the person the poem was about has switched places with another person without my noticing.

'Oh yes,' he says, not looking at me but at Georgs, who grasps the skin of the animal in one hand as if carrying the bunched train of a dress. 'Yes, yes.'

It is as if I am asking questions about a woman I've never met. I'm supposed to accept that my wife (a woman who ate so little meat that her doctor angrily diagnosed her as anaemic without even giving her blood tests, pronouncing the word 'vegetarian' as if she took it as a personal offence) went hunting. And I do accept it. Not only do I accept it but I'm hungry for it. I want more information, more stories, many more. More Leila, more Olaf. I want to bury myself neck-deep in the quicksand of grief. I want her to be taken more fully away from me, because at this moment she is still so close, so awfully close.

'Did she own a gun?' I whisper furiously at Olaf over his shoulder. He must feel my breath on his neck but says nothing, does not turn round.

'I need to help Georgs now,' he says, quietly. He

aims his statement at the animal. As Georgs hands over the knife to Olaf and turns away, Olaf takes it in his fist and jabs it at the air quickly, miming four little stabs into Georgs's lower back. He looks over at me as he does this and grins fiendishly. Georgs carries on walking.

I watch Olaf work at the carcass with sweat on his upper lip, his dirty jeans smeared with arterial blood, and I think about the poem in the letter, the girl walking through the city with flowers in her hair. He found the idea of a woman walking through the city with flowers in her hair to be beautiful, to be pertinent? To him? This man?

There's a different poem that has been haunting me. It's by Elizabeth Barrett Browning.

> 'I never gave a lock of hair away
> To a man, Dearest, except this to thee,
> Which now upon my fingers thoughtfully
> I ring out to the full brown length and say
> "Take it".'

Take it.

January 2002.
He was barely present. His eyes were dull, the long eyelashes fanning like a cow's tail in the grass.

In a certain light he looked so similar to me, in another not at all. In some ways I feel the same about my own reflection. Or photographs. How can that be me, I think, chancing upon some forgotten picture in among Petra's things, how can that ever have been me? I turn to a particular angle in the mirror and I practise saying positive things. Oh yes, I say. How interesting, I say. I do the Mona Lisa smile that Ina once taught me. She said it would help with my miserable face. I do the Mona Lisa smile and I say, fascinating. Tell me more. I'm so pleased. I'm so happy. So excited for you. I laugh a little bit, the way I've seen other women do it. The woman I want to be seen as doesn't throw her head back but simply parts her lips to allow the tinkling of glass to emerge. She mimics the sound of a fascinating dinner party being thrown in her honour. A hundred guests toast her beauty from the soft pillow of her tongue.

He made me swallow foreign objects and lie on my stomach and play dead. He said, you're dead, you can't move. He said, I can hear you breathing, shut up. I closed my eyes and died. It was easy to do.

The boar's hide hangs around its head and drapes on the ground beneath its body, like a marbled cloak. Here and there cling little patches of dark meat where they have cut too deeply. Olaf is drinking a beer now, leaning against a tree and watching Georgs, who takes his thin knife and cuts these pieces away. He tosses them on the ground for the dog, who has been going out of his mind throughout and falls upon them, throwing them to the back of his jaws and swallowing them without even chewing. When he is sated the dog comes and heaves his weight against my legs, burps and lies at my feet, his eyes twitching nervously in his head. Georgs takes the boar's head in his hands and cuts into it towards the neck with a heavier serrated blade, eventually twisting it loose and wrapping the whole thing in the skin, leaving nothing but the rubied stub of its neck, glistening.

I wander inside, since I feel my part in this disgusting play has come to its conclusion. After all, I killed the thing. It looks less impressive now that it is just meat. To think that I reduced it to that.

There isn't so much as a leg of lamb, a flayed side of beef, a bloodletting in all of art history that is not to some extent symbolic of human suffering. The rituals of death are the same. Both butchers and those who perform sacrifices are called *mageiros* in Greek. The only difference in their representation in iconography is that those who sacrifice are shown to wear twigs in their hair. I would like it if there were something of the forest left in our hair or on our clothes. Not only would it mean that the things that we were doing had meaning, it would also define our responsibilities.

The Calydonian Boar in Greek mythology is a huge, tempestuous beast that was set loose to ravage the lands. Most famously it is portrayed in Rubens' painting of the hunt that eventually felled it. Rubens' boar is almost as tall as the heroes that slay it. The thing that I hit with the car wouldn't stand up to a landscape. It would be swallowed by a swathe of a rider's cloak, or the shadow cast by a horse. Of course, death is not as glorious as Rubens would have us believe. He sold those scenes to punters who didn't have the money or the space for tapestries but nonetheless wanted something with which to intimidate guests. I prefer the other fleshes of his work. It's easy to see how similarly he treats all living things: how much excess blood he pumps through their systems, how he insists on gorging them so that their skin is taut around the belly, the paces he has put them through to leave their skin flush and their muscles tense. There is an appalling amount of life at stake.

I pour myself some wine and think about heading to my room for a nap, but Agnes has heard the door shut behind me and comes sashaying into the room. She smiles slyly and leans the side of her forehead against the door frame, bringing up a hand to toast me with her glass. I politely lift my own towards her with a smile and take a sip. She leaves her hand in the air, watching me for some reason. I don't know where to look and so stare with mute fascination into the drink, watching a stray crumb of cork bobbing here and there. Eventually she takes a mouthful of the wine and grins with slightly grey teeth at me as she swallows.

'So you're a big hunter now, yes?'

'Well, yes, it looks like it,' I say.

'You don't know how to butcher?'

'I once taught myself how to scale and clean bass by watching a YouTube video. That's a bit more straightforward though.'

Agnes nods slowly, and licks a droplet of wine from the edge of her glass.

'A fish.'

'Yes, a fish.' There's a crackle as a large furred moth lands in the yellow dome of the lamp just above my head. 'I imagine I could give it a go, you know. Now I've seen Georgs do it, I mean. The boar.'

'Where is your friend?'

'Ursula?'

Agnes shrugs elaborately. She leans back against the kitchen counter and tries to catch a hair from her tongue for what seems like a desperately long time, while making eye contact with me.

I say again, 'Do you mean Ursula?'

'Yes,' she says slowly, as if talking to someone of very limited mental capacity. 'I mean Ursula. Where is that lady? She's building a hotel here. Soon I'll be serving cocktails to lots of people. There will be motorbikes.'

I don't bother questioning her ideas on tourism. Instead I shake my head and say that I haven't heard from Ursula and that she could be in Riga. Agnes pretends to spit on the floor, but in doing so I notice that some spittle is actually released into the air in a fine spray and I flinch. She smiles.

'Riga is full of English people.'

'On motorbikes?'

'What?'

I look at my glass, which is empty, and Agnes moves to take it from me. She disappears and I am left alone in the room.

Ursula. I think of her sinewy forearms, the particular smell at the pit of her neck. A collection of sweat, perfume, the implication of intimacy that I had forgotten was open to me. Did I think that I could possibly survive being widowed? Yes. I thought about my life stretching out in front of me, a purely intellectual plain, stripped of the drinking holes of kisses, an aridity that I didn't altogether find hostile. Perhaps I considered my newly instated chastity as the correct realignment of the planets. As a young man I was most attractive to older women, and I enjoyed an affair or two at school via some meagre, maudlin charm and a pretentiousness that, with my white socks, they found amusing. However, when I finally cast aside the chubby hands and vulgar humour of my Italian teacher at the age of fifteen in the mistaken belief that there were more appropriately aged (and more attractive) women who would want to playfully shake my penis, I soon realised that the girls I had been thinking of found me boorish and too short. I spent a further ten years without so much as a glimpse of an exposed breast, patronising my own genitalia and ploughing through volumes of condensed, torturous poetry.

Inevitably, I became an academic, and at twenty-five fucked silently through what I considered to be my reformed virginity with a committed but mute air. When I found Leda it was a relief. We weren't drawn to each other in a way that other people would describe as passionate. What I mean is that we fell into bed after drunkenly talking for hours, and that it was this talking that was the real consummation of our feelings towards each other. It carried on like this. Though we made love pretty regularly, it was the hours beforehand that I (and I think she) took most pleasure in. The great, tortured act of foreplay was our conversation. And the drink, obviously. We both drank like fish. I can count on one hand the number of times we had sex soberly.

★

My failure to perform with Ursula may have put her off completely. I haven't heard from her although she took my number and kissed me goodbye. When I left her cabin I walked through the white morning along the beach with the fine salt collecting in my eyelashes and the waves coming in to swallow my footprints. I took off my shoes and tied them around my neck and rolled my trouser legs up so that I could fully experience the textures of the morning as it unfolded. I was cold and extremely sad. I mourned the death of the night with Ursula, which had held so much potential, the potential to arrest my obsession with Leda and Olaf and allow me to simply continue to live. I felt in every grain of sand that rubbed raw the skin of my toes the ghost of her feet walking this same path. I recalled a dream I'd had, of Olaf dragging behind him a purple, skinned animal. When I got close I saw that he was dragging Leda by her ankle, her hair darkened by the sea foam, her tongue swollen in her mouth, her skin softened by the brine.

As an experiment I try saying her name aloud to myself, first her name as I had known her: Leda, Leda, Leda over and over again, like a mantra given to me whose purpose is to align me with the primordial hum. Then, when that doesn't work because it becomes monotonous and meaningless, I do the same with her name as it had been before

I knew her: Leila, Leila, Leila. I feel an erotic charge when I say her name this way, as if she is someone new, someone strange, and therefore exciting in the way that my wife, the known lover, could never be. Perhaps it would be more accurate to say it is like hearing the name of my wife said by someone else. The someone who says it is a stranger with an accent that I cannot place: the idea of who she was is made new and startling by this new shape of the mouth.

I call Anne and the phone rings several times; I imagine it echoing in the hall of her house, where I have been many times, where I have had some of the most generously banal evenings of my life, discussing art or – more likely – bitching about our colleagues. I hovered in the hallway at parties to take advantage of the comforting prop of bookcases to ease myself into conversations, while Leda easily sank into the smallest gaps left by strangers and provided the punchlines to their jokes. The house is empty now and Anne elsewhere, and Leda will never ricochet her laugh from between the antique mirrors again.

November 2002.
I lie on my stomach and watch two things on the washing line: a white sheet and a white bra. The wind lifts them up

*and puts them down again. It is indifferent to the things
that they have touched and held and wrapped around. To
the wind they are cloth. They are nothing. There are days
when I can be the wind and the things that happen are
the clothes on the line. But there are other days when they
tangle around my legs and trip me up. I know there is a
correct way to hang the clothes on the line. My therapist
says it is the only way to stop tripping up, to simply line
them up and pin them, to acknowledge them as solid
objects that I could trip over. You are the wind, she says.
But you are a person too. She says it very carefully. She
knows that I don't like to be accused of being a person.*

Ursula returns from Riga and calls. She tells me
that I should get ready so that I can accompany
her on her trip up and down the coast, looking for
somewhere suitable for the resort that she has in
mind. It isn't a request. I have nothing much to do
and want to spend more time with her. In truth, I
had been wanting to reach out to her but failed to
think of the correct way to do it. She takes the onus
off me by first leaving for Riga and then calling
upon her return.

She picks me up early in the morning, leaning on
the horn to signal her arrival. I think that there is
a knowingness in the way she side-eyes me in the
car. She is reaching out to me, although she keeps

her conversation with me clipped and leans her cheek away from mine when I kiss her in greeting. She allows me to roll several cigarettes for her in the car. I line them up on the dashboard and wait for her to notice how straight and even they are, how unwrinkled the paper, how consistent the roll. However, she just reaches for them without taking her eyes from the road and carelessly puts them to her lips.

It seems as if every place we pass is suitable for a project of the kind she has in mind, each plot of land being flat, next to the sea and nestled in the forest, accessible by car but private. But Ursula sees something objectionable in each place. One is too easy to find, the next is too difficult, and in another she is convinced that the roof of a nearby paper factory would be visible at a certain angle from the prospective second floor. I begin to suspect that she has come here just to look at parcels of land and conjure up reasons to dismiss them. Once I am convinced of this I can just enjoy the drive, and her company, which is gregarious and funny. I even join in with the game at a property just outside Pitsrags.

'This place isn't right,' I volunteer, 'for a number of reasons.'

Ursula looks up at me with a smile. 'That's true,' she says, her eyes flashing, 'that's obvious.'

We talk as she drives. She loosens up as the hours

pass and I find she is especially receptive to talking about her work, despite her earlier protestations that she was glad to leave it behind. There is a moral vacuum for me that I know begins and ends at the perimeter of the forest, I say. I have evidence from my own studies that it is something universal, but Ursula tells me that my experience is narrower than I think. I say to her what about fairy tales, what about the wolves that eat the pigs, the wolves that get hunted here? Ursula smiles and winds down her window to throw some bit of thread or hair out onto the road. Then she winds it back up and glances sideways at me.

'That's not how it is,' she says. 'The wilderness represents a refuge. I've spoken to women here who see the wolves, the trees, as allies. The natural world protects, and the social world destroys. That's what children are taught here. Many of their grandparents took refuge in the forests during the war. It's a combination of folklore and real history. Do you understand?'

'I don't,' I say. 'To me the wilderness has nothing to do with being safe.' This is true. My feelings towards the wild landscape that surrounds us have been formed by so many years of storytelling. When I step through it, there are parts of me that are tugged through my skin by nettles and thorns and rearranged that way, like a cat's cradle. The wolves are waiting to lie to me and steal the things that I have brought to my grandmother, that sick lady. Things that I don't understand hide in the shadows. There are open traps waiting for me to press my feet against them so that they can be ripped from my legs. Weren't you told these stories, I ask? Ursula doesn't say anything. She keeps driving.

A truck in front of us is shedding shredded tissue paper. It spins in the air like feathers. I wonder whether Ursula can see where she is going. I think for an instant that we are being smothered from above. I feel the air closing around my face. I panic, my lungs refusing to take in enough air so that there is an enormous pressure around them although the thing that is causing it is literally nothing: paper, the wind, a whiteness in the air that would dissolve in the rain. Eventually we overtake it. I wonder whether Ursula noticed the change in my breathing, whether she thinks of me as someone who would be prone to nervous attacks. I cannot stop thinking about the night we spent together and about her judgement of me, about the way I have both failed to remain faithful to Leda and failed to properly accomplish my faithlessness. But the only things I can bring myself to talk about are academic.

I pull down the sun visor hoping for a mirror. I stare at myself for reassurance that I look composed, normal. Ursula fills the silence by telling me a story about an old woman she knows who lives just outside Riga in a chichi apartment with several cats (who aren't house trained but are, in whatever way, endearing). The old woman told Ursula that as a girl she had hidden a basket of figs in a beehive and the soldiers had found it. What were they doing looking in the beehive? The story makes no sense to me. Anyway, Ursula says, ignoring my question, there was a young wolf at the edge of the forest, and on seeing it, the old woman, who was a young woman at the time, had taken it as an omen and had walked in the opposite direction for several miles until she was so tired she had to curl up under a tree and nap. When she returned, the soldiers had taken her basket of figs and destroyed the hive by setting it alight or by crushing it with their boots. Now she lives in a chichi apartment, I say. What's the problem? Ursula shakes her head. Are the figs a metaphor for something, I ask? She says, no, the figs are food, and the food was stolen from her, and she was very hungry. The wolf protected her. It wasn't a grandma in disguise.

'Actually, in the story it is the *wolf* who is disguised as a grandmother.'

She frowns. When I try and elicit more conversation from her, she tells me that she is 'concentrating on the road' and I know that this is a metaphor for her being angry with me. Ursula is a very angry person, and I find this appealing. My parents internalised their rage and encouraged me to do the same. Leda and I wouldn't fight, because she said that she was 'allergic' to confrontation. It's true that whenever she got upset large red blotches would appear on her chest and neck and a red V would emerge as if branded onto her forehead. She would look as if she were choking on something. It unnerved me. I would retreat and leave her to it. Her anger seemed a private thing that I was embarrassed to witness. I want to ask Ursula whether I behaved in the correct way with Leda, because it has just occurred to me that I may not have – not only when she was angry but at various different times during our marriage. But I realise that now might be the worst time to ask for retrospective consolation for how I behaved in my marriage. And that Ursula would not want to discuss it. I make a mental note to ask her at a more appropriate time.

We park the car after a couple of hours next to a large red metal structure and agree to walk for half a mile or so along the beach. I mentally refer to the metal structure as 'a lighthouse' but it is more like a watchtower. We stand at the bottom of it and look up. It has a ladder all the way to the top and the red paint is peeling off it in great chunks. At the top is a platform. After a few seconds' consideration, Ursula puts her bag down on the sand and starts to climb the ladder. It sways and protests with a mechanical moan. I stand mutely praying that she'll change her mind so that I don't have to follow her up there and pretend to admire the view. Fortunately she does. She leaps down and brushes the sand from her hands and says to me, 'It's too dangerous,' and I nod, my heart beating wildly. Then we start to walk.

'How is the hunt going?' she asks.

I don't say anything, rather let out a dismissive lungful of air that is completely silenced and absorbed by the wind coming in from the sea. In a voice that feels too big for my mouth, I say, 'Fine.' I can't stand to raise my voice and I resent the landscape for demanding more from me than I am willing to give. This feeling evolves into feelings of resentment for Ursula herself, whose voice (did I imagine it?) lilts in irony when she says that word, 'hunt'. Then I change my mind and say, 'We shot a black wolf, you know.'

Ursula says, 'Oh?'

'Yes. We shot it but we didn't kill it.'

'Who's we, anyway?'

'Olaf and I.'

'It must have been a funny sort of gun for you both to have pulled the trigger.'

I stop walking and she rolls her eyes.

'I'm just kidding. Anyway, you know what I meant. Your hunt.'

'I feel that Olaf isn't telling me everything. But I don't know what it is that I want him to tell me.'

'You should be wary of Olaf,' Ursula says. She looks at me out of the corner of her eye. 'There must be some reason your wife never mentioned him. Never answered his letters. If she were alive you could ask her to explain. But since she isn't, perhaps you'd be better off trusting her judgement.'

'I sometimes wonder if Leda told me about it all and if I just wasn't listening. If I was trying to read or get to sleep. There must be a hundred things she told me while I was trying to do something else. I could have missed anything at all.'

'You don't honestly believe that she told you, of course.'

'No,' I say, 'but the thought occurs to me.'

'Were you a neglectful husband, do you think?'

'No,' I say. 'Unless I was.'

The wind whips the hair away from Ursula's collar and burns the cigarette that she is smoking down to nothing in the time that it takes for her to bring it to her mouth inside a uselessly cupped hand. After a few minutes we happen along some sort of large white bird that is standing at the edge of the water and looking out. It turns as we approach it and walks in front of us, now and again stopping and turning to us with a lugubrious eye. Ursula gets bored and runs towards it for a second or two, making it spread its wings and lift itself up above the sand for a foot or two before gliding down again. It is not a swan but something uglier and squatter.

Tiring of the biting wind and the endless white sand, we turn into the forest. There is a slight clearing and a couple of houses that look to me to be expensively built and seemingly unoccupied. Ursula says that they are probably holiday homes. The path widens and we start to go uphill. It is a relief to me to find some variant in the architecture of the ground, that there is interruption in the vastness of my surroundings. After several minutes we come to the crest of a hill and to a lean-to filled with chopped wood. Out of the side come pummelling three thin blond puppies. They launch themselves, barking and wagging their stiff tails, at Ursula, who laughs and drops her bag so that she can fully attend to the dogs. Two of them in particular are so overjoyed to see her that I am worried they are going to hurt her. The biggest leaps and drags its claws down the front of her dress while the other puts its jaws around her thin wrist. They are so young they haven't learned how to curb their energy, yet they are clearly going to grow into sizeable, strong animals. Even as babies they wield a clumsy ferocity that shines in their black eyes and tenses in the muscles beneath their grubby fur.

'Poor things,' Ursula says, after they have finished wrestling with her and lie at her feet panting. There is a ripped sack of bread inside the lean-to, which I point out. I say that I remember a childhood friend's springer spaniel once taking a hot roll, dripping with butter, straight from my hand at the dinner table and eating it in two exultant bites. Ursula shakes her head, unsatisfied.

'They need their mother,' she says, looking down at the dogs and gesturing mournfully. 'They're bored.'

She says it as if to be bored were the most desolate state imaginable.

After we have walked a little further, Ursula turns to me and kisses me on the mouth. Her lips part and I can feel her tongue. I hold her with my hands against her shoulder blades, and she holds me with her hands behind my elbows, as if she is saving me from a strong current. We hold each other like this for a while. Then we retrace our steps back to the car. Ursula takes her shoes off and then her trousers and lays them on the back seat. Then she lies on top of them, using the shoes for a pillow, and I give her head, or whatever the hell the term is for doing it to a woman. She is completely silent and I wonder if there is something that I should be doing that I'm not. Then she comes and grabs my head and makes a beautiful sound. I keep my mouth on her and we stay very still.

December 2003.

I saw my therapist today. She wants me to set a date for telling Seb about Leila. I mean, about me being Leila. I said that I would but then I kept coming up with excuses for why it couldn't be next week, couldn't be next month, wouldn't it really be better to wait for the new year, etc. She just stared blankly at me and said whatever I think is best, but I know she's disappointed in me. The truth is that I just don't think it matters particularly, I said. Imagine me asking Seb to sit down in the living room and asking him to wait there while upstairs I squeeze my feet into a pair of shoes that I had worn as an eleven-year-old, a pair of yellow patent sandals with a slight heel and a strap that closes around the back of the ankle. Slowly I make my way down, the heels clicking on the hard wood of the stairs, the toe pinching the side of my foot. In agony I present myself to my husband and say, Seb, I once cried in the bathroom because I wasn't able to dance in these shoes, and then later I saw Anna, the most beautiful girl at school, kissing an older boy and she was barefoot, and when I got home that night I threw the shoes out of the window. When my mother found them in the gravel at the front of the house in the morning she ran upstairs and pulled the sheets off me and hit me with them, saying 'Spoilt! Spoilt! Spoilt!'

and that was the last thing she said to me for two weeks. Imagine me saying Seb, I wanted you to see me in these shoes, and imagine my husband looking at me, and saying 'Why?' Well, I said, that's what I think about telling Seb about Leila. Because you think he wouldn't understand? she asked me. No, I said. Because it's none of his business.

'Do you think you're spoilt?' my therapist asked me. I just smiled wryly. Oh please, I said. I like to identify when she is doing Therapy at me and just let her know that I know. If I'm paying her all this money I at least want her to know that I think I am being swindled out of it.

I have been barefoot on two memorable occasions in my life since seeing Anna kiss an older boy. Once was on hot sand and the other was on a wet street. On both occasions I thought about her and on both occasions I felt sad because I bet she wasn't thinking about anything, only kissing and being kissed. I'm so much older than she was, though. It's impossible for my moments to exist in isolation from those that have come before.

On the hot sand I was picked up and carried to the water by a handsome man who worked at the hotel. He picked me up and carried me because the sand was burning my feet. But he also picked me up and carried me because we were having a silent affair. I knew we were having a silent affair from the moment that I watched him carry my suitcase up the stairs. I didn't see him again until the following morning. Seb was sleeping off a headache. I was trying to walk on the hot sand. I wasn't wearing any shoes. I hopped on the balls of my feet and the man who worked at the hotel ran towards me and scooped me up like a pat of butter. First he held my suitcase in his hands and then he held me! I could smell the sweat on his chest. It spread in a damp fist-shaped patch over his heart. That's all that happened. But it was an affair, and I thought about Anna kissing the older boy.

And I thought about her on the wet street, too.

They're stained, these moments, they drag their feet through dye and are stained, and they track the dye through the house and up the stairs and under the sheets of my bed.

I'm pleased to see when we arrive at the house that Agnes's car is not in its usual position, meaning that she has had some business to attend to either in a neighbouring village or possibly even in town. However, as we step out of the car I see that there is somebody at the door. It is Georgs. He is slumped in the doorway, turned towards the house, possibly waiting for an answer to his knock, and his legs are buckled slightly. Ursula looks at me curiously.

'Georgs?' I say, walking towards him and tentatively reaching towards his shoulder to place my hand there. He is still a good five inches taller than me, even in this strange state. He turns towards me. His right eye contains a black penny. I've never seen an eye look such a way: almost sticky with black blood. Ursula is behind me and I hear her intake of breath.

'Oh,' she says, 'are you okay?'

Georgs bats my hand away but allows Ursula to talk to him briefly in Latvian. We help him into the house and he immediately starts ransacking the place for booze. I offer him wine but he looks at me as if I've said something that makes him wish he were dead rather than here. I understand this feeling. I would recognise it anywhere. I tell Ursula that he wants to get loaded and she says, 'Well, help him, then, for God's sake.' I smile at this because I know more than ever that she is a good person. I find two bottles of wine and some black balsam. There are pallets of the stuff, covered with an old oilskin tablecloth. Ursula makes a face at the bottle.

'Only old men drink that,' she says. But Georgs grins widely and slams his fist down on the table.

'Great!' he says. I pour three glasses and Ursula joins us in the pantomime of saying '*Prieka*' and clashing them together as if we were three old friends who have heard good news. She doesn't drink, but simply wets her lips. Then she leans forward and says something to Georgs, which I imagine must be about his eye as he reflexively prods beneath it. He shakes his head and smiles again, but his eyes – the black one and the other, which is as grey as the sky – are wet with tears.

'Somebody did this to him,' Ursula says. She is moved. I want to tell her that Georgs is a suspicious character, and that we should be careful about getting involved in whatever awful things are currently happening to him. However, I know this would be hard to articulate discreetly, especially since I have no solid evidence myself. Instead I busy myself with filling Georgs's glass and making concerned noises as Ursula talks to him. At one point I suggest that we drive him to the hospital, but Ursula says she has already suggested it and that Georgs refuses to go. I say that his eye looks pretty bad, that I've never seen an eye like that before.

'I have,' Ursula says. 'My brother once kicked a kitten that we found by the lake.'

I pretend to know which lake she is talking about.

'That's terrible,' I say.

'Actually he survived,' Ursula says, 'he just had this round black thing that would move around his eye. And he was slow, but we never knew whether that was my brother's fault or whether he was born that way.'

I turn back to the patient.

'Can you see?' I ask. He ignores me. 'I know you understand what I'm saying,' I say. Ursula pats Georgs's hand. 'I fucking hate this person,' I say to Ursula. 'I don't know why he's come to me for help.' Then it dawns on me that he is probably here

to see Agnes. 'Agnes isn't here,' I say. I point out of
the window towards the absence of her car. Georgs
turns and looks but doesn't seem overly concerned.
Actually he seems to be in pretty high spirits.
After one final drink he goes to leave and neither
Ursula nor I stop him, although I have a feeling
he should be lying in the recovery position rather
than wandering around. We watch him through the
window walking, or rather staggering, out of sight.

'He didn't have his dog with him,' I remark.

'I think I'd better go too,' she says. I walk her out
and watch as she starts her car. Before she can turn
to wave to me I shut the door with a terrible sigh.

Zeus impregnated Leda and she gave birth to an
egg. Out of the egg hatched two children. My wife
never once talked about children. We ended the
conversation once and for all the day that we had
the termination. She was such a generous person I
imagine that she found it difficult not to accept the
thing that was happening to her, to reject it instead. I
do feel residual guilt. I know that I shouldn't but I do.

August 2003.

Sometimes I stop for a minute before going into the
house and I sit on the front step with my keys in my fist.
The smell of onions frying escapes from a pan in the

*neighbour's kitchen and makes my teeth ache. Senses
have a way of doing this, of bleeding into each other.
One minute you are listening to the sound of the waves
breaking against the shore and the next you are choking
on tissue paper. What I'm trying to say is it's easy to
confuse one thing for another. My therapist asks me if I'm
feeling guilty or betrayed or angry or defensive and I just
say yeah, I think so, it's hard to tell. Another letter came
this morning.*

Since Georgs's visit, I have found Olaf is increasingly
difficult to pin down. He answers his phone and then
pretends not to understand me, or doesn't answer
it at all. I am convinced that he had something to
do with Georgs's injuries, but surmise (in order to
reassure myself) that they had a drunken fight. After
all, I have no allegiances. However, I can't help but
worry about Georgs. What if he has lost his sight?
I should have taken him to the hospital. I listened
to Ursula because her decisiveness and sanity are so
valuable to me in the midst of all this. On top of
that, I can't stop thinking about Olaf. I am equally
repelled by and attracted to him. He is the wound I
dig at until it scars.

Agnes isn't speaking to me and when I ask
her whether she knows where the men are, she
shrugs. The smell of my room is starting to turn

my stomach: a combination of wood varnish, the
sulphuric water that drips constantly from the tap
and stale oil from my solitary meals. I have been
avoiding the clubhouse and its excess of booze and
talk – much of which goes straight over my head –
but I decide I will take a last trip. Despite myself, I
also want to check on Georgs.

It's early at the club and Olaf is alone. He is counting
coins and lining them up along the table in front of
him in size order. I think he is listening to the horse
race that is being shown on the large TV, although
he is turned away from it. His face is cracked and
dark like the stone of a rotten peach. The sound of
the horse race is indistinct, so much so that I can't
tell whether it is being commentated on in Latvian
or Russian. It reminds me of Sundays as a child, of
lying down on a sofa with my face turned inwards
and my hair sticking uncomfortably to my temples
while the radio mumbled a horse race in the other
room. That restless feeling of being still. I look into
his face and try and see some semblance of Leda
there. I want him to take her place, for one minute,
for one second.

'Olaf, I must talk to you,' I say. He grunts and
holds up a finger.

'I have to listen. I might still win.'

'My father was interested in the horses. A big

gambler,' I say. He ignores me. After a while the
pitch of the commentary heightens and Olaf stares
in front of him as if possessed, the eyes jutting from
the skull. He swears.

'No luck?'

'My horse fell,' he says. 'What do you want?'

'I know you wrote to Leda often.'

'Yes.'

'Why didn't she write back?'

'How should I know?'

'But you do know. I'm sure you know.'

'She thought she was too good for us,' Olaf says.
Once again he won't allow his gaze to lift and meet
mine. I see his eyes like glossy darts aimed in front
of him, at his own palms. Could it be possible that
tears have started to form? He clenches his jaw and
I watch the muscles flinch. 'She forgot about us.'

'But you carried on writing to her for so long.
You must have loved her very much.'

'You know how I found out she was dead? In the
newspaper.'

'I'm sorry. I would have told you. I didn't know
you existed.' I say it again: 'She never mentioned
you.'

He slowly gets up from his chair and goes to turn
the TV to another channel and then another until
he finds something he likes. It is some live concert
or other, a recital of Bruch's violin concerto in G

minor. I smile in recognition. Olaf returns to the table. He carefully uses his left hand to pull the coins into the palm of the right and leans back in his chair. He closes his eyes to listen to the music. There is something that appeals to him, whether it is the sound of the music itself or nostalgia for something, I couldn't say. After all, it is difficult to separate these emotions within ourselves. He holds the coins in his fist and I can almost smell the metallic warmth of them. A crack appears between his lower and upper eyelids and he says, 'It reminds you of Leila.' It is a statement, not a question. I say yes, politely – that we liked a lot of music. The piece holds no special appeal for me but it is true to say that it reminds me of Leda, that everything does. He nods and we listen to the Allegro together.

'It reminds me,' he says. 'The way she would play her violin for such a long time. We could not get her to leave her room. She was at that age. Very serious.'

I sit and stare at Olaf. I watch with disbelief as he passes his hand over his brow, over his jutting nose and fleshy mouth, and finally smiles, with his hand hovering around his throat. A prickling sensation spreads across the palms of my hands and along my forearms. My fingers clench and unclench themselves. Does Olaf know what he is doing? Does he take pleasure in the telling of these secrets, extracting them like splinters from the white flesh of history? I look at him and see nothing, just a mask. He runs one finger around the collar of his shirt to allow air to pass between his skin and the cloth. I wait for him to speak as if he is a priest and I have done something wrong, a feeling I have had for so long that if I were a different person who believed in different things I would be convinced that I was paying for a crime I committed in another life.

I try and imagine Leda with her hand on the bow of a violin. It's impossible, though. I can see a girl like Leda, dark and with the skin under her eyes sitting thin and bluish, but it isn't Leda. It is more like her sister, or perhaps her ghost. My confusion renders me immobile, the figure of Olaf in his chair receding into a vibrating speck amid a screen of white noise.

I can hear her voice now whispering to me furiously, her body not moving an inch. We were sitting in the gods in Vienna, our necks craned. Our heads were bent in humiliation. The music had swollen and broken above us and we were just whelks being sucked from the safety of our shells. We were paralysed.

'Imagine how lovely it would be,' she had whispered to me then, 'to be musical.'

'Yes,' I replied. 'Yes, imagine.'

I saw her nostrils flutter as she breathed. As we had stepped inside the theatre, a man had placed his hand on hers in error, and through the very fabric of her coat against mine I had felt her thrill. We experienced these feelings in tandem, we turned in the same breath, we sighed together in the back of the car, we slept with our bodies touching that night and every night that followed it, except in the strangest, most exceptional circumstances. I bought her a violin the following week, had it delivered to the house and waited for her arrival, unable to sit down as the excitement acted like bolts in the bones of my legs. She came home late, exhausted, threw her bag down in the hall and then froze in the act of taking off her coat, the violin in its little coffin on the stairs, and me hovering by its side, trembling with anticipation, so pleased with myself.

'What is that?' she asked.

'A present,' I said.

'No, Seb,' she said. 'No. Please take it away.'

'But – Puccini. You said. I'll pay for lessons.'

'I can't,' she said. 'I can't. Please.'

But she could.

I feel it like a grenade in my throat. But I speak in measured tones and I police my movements so that they are well paced, so that the steady thrum of my heart acts as a metronome.

'What is this anyway?' I say. Olaf looks steadily at

me. I take the lock of hair out of my pocket and place it on the table. He smiles.

'Her beautiful hair,' he says.

'What?' I say. I'm starting to lose focus. 'You don't get to say "her beautiful hair", okay?'

'I was sending it back to her. I shouldn't have taken it.'

I involuntarily see his hands, nails broken to the quick, painful-looking shards at the end of grey, grasping fingers (though they were young then, and presumably he, like all of us, has his youth still hidden inside him, a beautiful secret that we are desperate to tell other people), and his neck, bruised-looking from neglectful shaving (but no, I have to make sure that I am completely in the moment as it happens, I have to imagine instead his head at the end of a neck that is creaseless and pale, the blue veins, vulnerable, his figure not yet bolstered by weight but in that ungainly stage of sinew, and features that are somehow too large for the face, for I imagine the lock of hair to be attached to a nine-year-old Leda, Leda as a child, Leila, a tiny thing, a beautiful thing of no consequence, a thing that hasn't happened yet), as he leans over to take the lock of hair, silently pinching it between his thumb and forefinger, the thief, the criminal.

'I see,' I say. I see.

'He wasn't good enough for her, he was useless, he

didn't deserve to have it.' Olaf seems to be speaking to himself now and I am embarrassed for both of us, the two men unravelling at the dirty table.

'What are you talking about?'

'Georgs. She sent it to him in a letter. I followed her and took the letter and I stole the hair from inside, he never knew it was there. It was mine. I deserved to have it.'

May 2004.

I start to write Seb a letter. It's something I have never done before. We talk all the time, we send texts and emails, I call him at the slightest provocation. I find while I'm writing the letter that I have taken on the voice of somebody else. I have become the person who would write a letter. I laugh because it sounds so ridiculous. But I have to write it down. In the corner of the letter I draw a rose. I know he loves my drawings, that he keeps every single scratch that my pencil makes. Then I simply tear out the rose and put it on his pillow. I throw the rest of the letter in the bin. I just don't feel connected to the things I have said.

What happened? What happened? I want to be specific with my truth. I want to cast out the demons that play with my hair while I sleep.

'I'm losing my mind here,' I say. There's a silence

on the other end. I have to stay completely still otherwise I lose the signal. 'Anne? Hello?'

'Yes, all right, hello, just give me a minute. I'm trying to process the information.'

I tell her that she has absolutely no right to process the information, that I'm here all alone and I just need to hear a familiar voice tell me that it's insane, it's a humiliation of the highest order, that I simply need to feel I am being listened to and understood.

'Well,' she says, slowly, 'I can hear that you're upset and I do understand.'

That's not really good enough, I say. That's about as much as I would expect from the Samaritans but not from an emotionally intelligent person such as herself. Then I realise that I'm inadvertently complimenting her, so I say, 'To all appearances.'

I don't want her to think that I think that she is a model of humanitarianism or anything. I only meant to cast aspersions on the Samaritans and the amount of good they do. Anyway, instead of recounting this for Anne I just breathe down the phone and Anne says it sounds like I have a cold.

'I don't have a cold,' I say, 'I just have a sinus thing.' Anne then says that if it makes me feel any better, she feels very unnerved about the whole situation as well, that Olaf sounds as though he might have some mental health problems at the very least. I interrupt her to say that I feel not betrayed exactly, but deeply sad to think that Leda had something that she felt the need to get so very far away from, and that she presumed we would not understand.

Anne says that she thinks that really I understood her very well, that Leda felt understood and accepted by me, and that we do not need to be forensic examiners in order to understand something, in order to love it. I say that makes me feel better and it does. It makes me feel better but it also makes me cry. I cry fat tears that surprise me by their voluptuousness, by the way they swell excessively over my lips and hang from my chin and I hold the phone away from my mouth and nose so that Anne can't hear that I'm crying and will presume that I'm just mouth breathing due to the sinus thing. I realise that my sinus thing isn't a thing at all, not an infection or an allergy as I might have thought, but the build-up of these tears over hours, days maybe, that the pain behind my eyes and at the top of my throat was grief.

'I think I've done all I can,' I say. 'It must be time to come back. I can leave right away. I should get back to work.' Anne clears her throat then and says, 'Listen,' and then after she is sure that I am listening and no longer crying, she tells me that I am fired. She phrases it differently. She says that *we're* (she uses the inclusive plural to comfort me) not looking to go any further with the (my) proposal. She is polite and I find she is using a soothing voice. I end the call and lie face down on my bed.

The resolution of the trip as I imagined it has been taken away from me. It's as if the tablecloth has been whipped from under me and I am standing alone now among the teapot and cups – still visibly the same but altered, subtly and irrevocably. I must now reimagine the return journey and the thing that waits for me at the end of it and come to terms with it. When Anne asked how my 'holiday' was going she had betrayed something that I was only faintly aware of myself, which was that the thing I was doing here, whatever it was, other people viewed as self-indulgent, as if I had taken a trip through the Champagne region, stopping only at the side of roads to piss fine wine into the dust. I believed I was researching. It's true that I found Ursula and that I kissed her and was now following her into Riga, hopefully to kiss her again and to go into churches, which I know she likes, and to eat plates of hot meat and smoked fish. But that has happened without my consent. I have been thrown off track. I have felt like an anthropologist, like Ursula, mutely following around a group of subjects, not to learn anything about them in particular, but because I want to learn about a lost member of their tribe, who seemingly had shrugged off one life in order

to begin again in another. In so many ways it feels as
if I have been chasing a mirage, and I am tired and
thirsty. What had seemed graceful and diaphanous
was actually more spectral.

October 2004.

*It's like the further away from me the terrible thing is, the
more it hurts me. At the time it was hard but I slept all
night and ate my breakfast in the morning. Now I feel
it tugging on me as if on a hair from a sunburned scalp.
It is distracting. I can't work. I can't think. I can't eat. I
thought that it would be enough to leave the country and
never look back. But it's lodged inside me. I can't lie still at
night. I hear things. Not noises but — is it possible to hear
what wire feels like? Is it at all possible that I can hear
the ice splitting and cracking? I mean all of it. Not just
the Arctic ice being destroyed but, closer, more devastating,
the ice sheet on top of a duck pond in a suburban garden,
the ice cube in a heavy-bottomed glass with a warm hand
wrapped around it. I can hear it. Every time I close my
eyes. I can feel things that aren't there. I am like the princess
and the pea. The hundreds of mattresses are the days that
I have tried to live, and that I have laid beneath me. I
have been ordered. I have been meticulous. I have 'made a
name for myself' in the most literal sense. I am the person
that I have insisted upon becoming. I'm no longer afraid of
betraying myself as being uncultured or parochial because*

I am not those things. I am an artist who has spent her entire adult life in this capital city and I deserve to sign my name Leda and speak my name Leda. If I wake up in the middle of the night inhaling sharply because it feels like something just rolled in between my ribs then I'll do what every other woman in this city would do, which is to drink too much and cry on my way to the supermarket.

There are no caves, no forests, just miles and miles of refrigerated aisles. I walk up and down them as if trying to solve a puzzle. The solution is milk. The solution is to pick up the kind of milk that has a circle of gold foil over the neck. The solution is to feel; every time I peel the gold circle from the neck, that I should put it in my pocket and carry it around with me like a coin, but to instead put it in the bin and carry nothing around in my pockets at all, because I know now that to carry things in one's pockets ruins the shape of the trousers, ruins the silhouette.

One thing I want to do before I leave is to find Georgs, but I have no idea where to start looking. Agnes is no help. I talk to Ursula on the phone and she reassures me that it is not my responsibility, but the image of his black eye shining like an eclipsed moon in the middle of his head reappears when I put my head on the pillow at night. I recall the image I had while walking on the beach of Olaf dragging a corpse behind him and I can't shake it. I lose sleep so that by the time morning comes I am exhausted and my brain rebels from the frightening things it has made itself see. I can't hold a conversation or a thought. I know that it is insane but I start to entertain the idea that Olaf might be somehow responsible for my wife's death.

When I open the door to leave the house there is a small black shrew outside. It is dead and waterlogged. I make an involuntary yelp at the sight of it, an embarrassing noise that escapes my lips from some differently pitched place inside of me, a place which acts like a bicycle horn when pushed. Agnes shoves past me and picks the shrew up by its tail, flinging it like a rotten apple into the undergrowth.

'Cats,' she says. I nod, slowly, but I am simply humouring her. I know that it is a sign, that it is a violent act that must be attributed correctly to its perpetrator.

For several days I find myself falling into an unchanging pattern of behaviour. I start very early each morning. I do not wash, but instead climb into the same clothes I discard each night, descend the stairs and close the door quietly behind me. I cannot explain exactly what I am doing. I just have the feeling all over me, all the time, that I must see Olaf.

I walk at a swift pace, as if I'm running late for the event that is his presence in front of me. When I reach the path that leads to his house I crouch down and I wait for him. All I can see is the silhouette of him moving around inside the yellow square of the kitchen window, but it is enough. My breath slows. I rock from side to side to keep the blood flowing through my feet.

By the time I get back to the house I am starving. I eat bread torn straight from the paper bag and stick my head under the tap in a way that I haven't done since I was a child. Then I wash and eat a second breakfast, either alone or with Agnes.

I keep expecting to be caught, though I'm not exactly sure what it is I'd be caught doing. In fact, the only thing that happens is that one morning I come to the path and see that Olaf is standing facing the window. I am startled to see his square face, his forehead appears to be resting against the glass, his two hands, palms forwards, either side of it. It looks as if he is looking out into the world and I am convinced that it is me he expects to see, but as I get closer, slipping into the slender gap between a metal bin and the front wall, I can see that his eyes are shut. He is motionless and unseeing, lost in some thought or action that is meaningless to me. Something like a prayer.

There has been no precedent for the way I am behaving. I am naturally drawn to the quiet order of living unremarkably. When it comes to my forays into the world I am something like a hermit crab, finding intellectual and spiritual solace in things that don't belong to me.

The letters are damp and creased in my pocket. I carry them everywhere with me. I do not change my shirt. The air in the forest has been breathed through the lungs of so many trees it reaches me glistening and gurgles down the plughole of my throat.

Agnes is waiting for me one morning as I skulk through the kitchen, my stinking shirt lying heavily across my chest, my breath unconsciously held as I try and cross the threshold of the house and escape into my strange morning ritual. She is dressed already, her hair in a complicated plait across her head, her nails shaped and brightly coloured, flashing as she pokes one at my chest and demands that I go back upstairs immediately and change. There is a birthday party being thrown for a friend of hers in a neighbouring town, and she wants me to drive her there. Actually the party is being thrown for the friend's young daughter. Agnes has made a sour cream cake that she has put in a white box with a large chiffon bow around it. It sits on the counter primly.

I reluctantly wash at my sink upstairs and put on new clothes, clothes that have been folded for so long in my suitcase that they are heavily lined, almost as if new. This reminds me of how long I have been here, trapped of my own accord. I help carry the cake to the car and we begin the long drive, with Agnes pointing out the way from memory. Her instructions are staccato and often come at the last minute as she suddenly recognises a turn in the road or a shortcut. She keeps saying that I'll like this woman, because she's been on TV.

'Is she an actress?'

'No. Her house was flooded and a family of beavers moved into the kitchen.'

'She was on TV for that?'

'She was interviewed by the news on every channel!'

She has put on lipstick very precisely in a shape that isn't quite that of her mouth. We stop off at the nearest shop and I get out of the car to help load crates of beer into the back. Coming out as Agnes goes in is Georgs, carrying a plastic bag with a bottle inside it. They exchange a few words and he turns to look at me. I shout his name. He makes his way over. He seems agitated. He doesn't make eye contact and shifts the bag from one hand to the other. When I see Georgs his dog normally sniffs the palms of my hands in an obscene manner. Therefore I reflexively fold my arms across my chest. But today Georgs is on his own. It crosses my mind that I've never seen him exist by himself before. It turns out that this is what's troubling him. He is on his way to find the dog, who is lost, or has been stolen, or has run away. I look at the black thing that his eye has become. I feel responsible for it, for some reason. I offer to help find the dog but Georgs looks at me uncomprehendingly. He simply says, 'No.' I glance at my watch and make a solemn promise to myself that I will be back at the house at a reasonable time, to complete the tasks that I set for myself this morning. These tasks are, namely, to get things in order and to prepare to leave. Then I insist that Georgs get into the back of the car. When Agnes comes out carrying her purse in her fingertips and walking on her tiptoes like a cartoon character, she protests at Georgs's presence. I tell her that I have to help find the dog and she sulks that I won't be coming with her to the party, no doubt hoping that my presence at her side would be misconstrued as romantic.

On the way I ask Agnes to translate for me as I ask Georgs questions about the dog, but she is prepping herself for the party and isn't interested. Every so often she checks to see that Georgs isn't squashing the cake or drinking her beer supply in the back. In fact he is miserably sucking from his own bottle of booze. I can't see what it is but the car stinks of it. I keep thinking of what Olaf said, but it's impossible for me to believe that this rotten, broken thing slumped behind me was once Leda's boyfriend. If Olaf is to be trusted at all – which I am starting to doubt.

'Ask him where he last saw the dog,' I say.

'He says that Olaf took him out hunting.'

'Where is Olaf? I need to speak to him. Can you try calling him?'

Agnes sighs dramatically and snaps her compact mirror shut. She digs her phone, an ancient thing, out of her handbag and dials the number.

'Do you want to speak to him?'

'No,' I say, 'I'm driving. Just ask him where we should start to look.'

Agnes gets through to Olaf and speaks to him briefly.

'He says that you should go to the Peldarga Caves. Here, I'll show you on the map. It's not far away. Olaf will meet you there.'

'I'm starting to wish I'd never met him.'

'Oh, don't be silly. I believe he used to be a good man, a handsome young man. He drinks too much now. It's very sad. But you should be kinder to him. You've both lost the same person after all.'

I ignore Agnes and instead make eye contact with Georgs in the rearview mirror.

'Peldarga Caves?' I say. He nods, yes, he knows where they are. Soon we are at the house and I practically shove Agnes out of the car.

'How do I look?' Agnes asks before she shuts the door.

'A million dollars,' I say. There are shouts and screams from excited children in the garden of the house. Agnes carefully takes the cake from the seat next to Georgs and a fat man with a white handlebar moustache puts his arm round her.

When we reach our destination, some thirty minutes away, Olaf is waiting at the side of the road. He is leaning against the bonnet of his car, smoking a cigarette, sheltering it from the wind with his hand around the lit end like something very fragile.

'What the hell are we doing here?' I ask.

'Georgs,' he says in a sing-song voice, 'I know where your dog is, Georgs.' He uses his fingers to stroke the underside of Georgs's chin as if he himself is a beloved animal. Olaf's car is parked haphazardly. Wordlessly, Georgs climbs in. He is like a zombie.

'Where are we going?' I ask. Olaf simply rubs out the cigarette on the roof of the car and then smiles conspiratorially. 'Shall I leave the car here?'

'Yes,' he says. 'It will be fine. We will come back for it. But you must come.'

'Why?'

'You will see, Seb!' This is only the second time Olaf has used my name and it goes off like a shotgun in my head, the aviary of my thoughts scattering.

I check that Agnes's car is locked and reluctantly get into the front seat of his, whose engine he has kept running. It is warm inside, musty-smelling, and the seats feel very low to the ground so that every pebble under the wheels judders through my skull. After only a few minutes, Georgs has fallen asleep with a small hard leather bag underneath his head. His snores reverberate in the car and I have the feeling that we are delivering him, like a devoted service animal at the end of his life, to the needle of a vet. His throat incubates the sound before it leaps wetly through his flared nostrils. Olaf taps the steering wheel and lurches to both sides to check the wing mirrors, the car lurching in turn.

We pull up on a gravelled patch of land at the side of the forest. The stars are out and they are magnificent, throwing pale ochre and green cloaks around themselves, gossiping. We are about five hundred metres upstream from Dundaga, at the mouth of the Peldarga Caves. I ask Olaf whether he is sure the dog is inside the caves. He smiles broadly. Yes, he says. Absolutely the dog is in the caves. If it is, I think, it's only because you have driven it there. I wake Georgs up by tapping on his shoe with my fist.

Outside the cave I hear a sound. It is like the sound of the wind passing over the neck of a bottle, but it is also the sound of dogs howling, or that of a hundred lonely ghosts. It is the wind breaking the branches of the trees and howling from the carapace of the cave. I am standing on the cusp of something truly wild and not meant for me.

Georgs steps, at Olaf's urging, into the cave, guiding himself with nothing but the weak light from his phone. Olaf dances from one foot to the other at the precipice, allowing only his voice to teasingly follow. I am angry, mostly at Georgs, who allows Olaf to bully and manipulate him, although as I feel the singing anger make its way through my bloodstream I realise that I am no better – no better than Olaf, as I have inexplicably hated Georgs from the moment that I met him, and refused to help him even in a time of great physical distress, but also no better than Georgs, as I follow Olaf from pillar to post waiting for him to drop shreds of information that I hungrily devour from the floor of the forest. Did I really believe we would find Georgs's dog here at all, or am I under the spell of this madman, trailing after him like a scarf in the dirt?

Georgs is out of sight now. Olaf grabs my shoulder with one hand.

'We have him now, we have him,' he says to me. His breath spits hotly against my ear.

I say, 'We have to help him. He can't see. For God's sake.'

'We'll kill him,' Olaf says. His eyes are heaving

from their sockets. 'I know you want to kill him.' It seems to me as if he is twice as large as he has ever been, as if he is engorged from some bilious disease, and the feel of his hand, heavy on my shoulder, is sickening to me.

'I'll take him in very deep,' he says, 'and I'll leave him. You don't have to do it. We'll scare him. Just scare him a little.' He draws something with his finger in the air. I shake my head. I ask him what is wrong with him. He stares at me with an absolute lack of expression on his potholed face. It is like looking for meaning in a headstone whose dates have been washed away by years of rain. I break my gaze from his.

I walk silently into the dark. I follow the noises that Georgs makes. It is extremely cold inside the caves. Where the light touches the walls, it glints from water thinly trickling and from creeping, colourless mosses. As I get deeper I hear that Georgs is no longer calling for his dog but shouting my name in faltering bursts. It echoes sorrowfully along the walls. I stumble through the dim passageway, my breath in my ears, hallucinating the feel of feral things running up the legs of my trousers and across my back, until I reach him. I stretch my hand out to him and he grasps at it, clutching the ends of the fingers and losing his footing. He falls against the wall and hits his head with a dreadful crack that makes all the blood rush from my extremities and concentrate itself in my heart.

'Georgs,' I say, the sound of my own voice returning with an alien reverberation, my shout captured and thrown back at me with frightening force. I pick Georgs up from the cave floor, his clothes so cold they feel sodden to me, and I half-carry him. He talks to me in garbled Latvian and I simply apologise, over and over again.

Do I invent again that howling, could Georgs's dog really be in here somewhere with us? Could wolves take refuge here? I imagine the black wolf that the men shot in the forest, its fur slick with bright oxygenated blood, its eyes yellow moons, panting, waiting for us, knowing that we would be drawn somehow in this direction, by an uncontrollable urge to receive the punishment that we were due. Like a pious monk I carry Georgs in my open arms and beg a greater power to receive us.

The darkness is a room that only we inhabit, less a colour than a feeling, a loneliness – for me nothing less than the reminder that unsafe spaces still exist, are waiting to engulf us whole, if we are only able to bring ourselves to step into them.

At the mouth of the cave, which is blue in contrast, a curtain of royal blue, I hesitate. The weight of Georgs is unbearable. Outside I know that Olaf is silhouetted somewhere, a golem among the pines.

The muscles in my arm strain as Georgs starts to lurch forward. I'm claustrophobic, overwhelmed by his closeness, his weight dragging my shoulder from its socket, his jerking, the moans that escape his broken-looking mouth. What if I hadn't been there when he had fallen? What if I was never here at all? I so easily could have been somewhere else, so plausibly could have never been anywhere near, never stepped foot in the caves. If it hadn't been for me, would he have fallen and never stood up again? I allow my grip to loosen and the fabric of his jacket slides wetly through my fingers. Where is Olaf? I will myself to say his name but it barely escapes my throat. I choke on it. I can't bear Georgs any more. The impulse to withdraw my body from his is overwhelming. I shove him sharply away from me and he staggers towards the road. The headlights of Olaf's car light up in the dark so fiercely that I close my eyes. The engine roars into life. I have delivered Georgs to this moment. I have done this.

The car stops suddenly and I feel, rather than hear, the familiar soft, wet thud of the boar hitting the bumper. Except, of course, that it is Georgs's body that makes the sound. I was right to think of this moment as a punishment. To think that these events were destined to transpire. I simply inhale the sharp, thin air and the sweet scent of pine needles and exhaust fumes. In the distance I can hear two owls calling to each other, desperately calling. The sound of the wind echoes through the cave. It is as if someone is standing behind me, pressing the flat of his hand against one ear and then the other. The car door is heaved open. Olaf runs towards me. His boots stomp relentlessly into the hard earth. He wheezes maniacally. When he reaches me he clutches at my shirt and pulls himself forward, holding the side of his head against my chest, which beats with the steady thrum of my startled heart.

'I know you watch me, don't you, Seb?' he murmurs. 'But you hide from me. You fear me.' He rocks back and forth, still holding me like a mother clutching on to her baby. I have to fight to keep my balance. His hands creep upwards towards my throat, and they hold me like that, his fingers touching around the back of my neck and under my hairline. I thrust my fists into his huge chest and heave myself away from him. His hands let go of my throat – so lightly, so quickly, that they might never have been there at all. We face each other, catching our breath, and his smile glows thinly like a crescent moon.

Olaf's face is inches from mine. I can see that he is weeping now. His eyes are shining. It is ridiculously beautiful in the starlight.

'Do you think she sees us?' he says.

'Who?' I say, although I know.

'Oh my God,' he cries. 'Do you think she sees what we do?'

December 2004.

We bought a tree today. We were late and so the ones that were left were haggard and thin. I felt pity for them. Seb made fun of me. He said, all these trees are your children. We named them. The salesman asked if he could help. Seb said, yes. Please gather all these orphan trees together. My wife has made mittens for them. The salesman said, I don't understand. We chose a tall tree. We hid its bald patches easily by turning it against the wall. We are always so generous with gifts. Especially Seb. He communicates through material things.

I feel anxious in the pit of my stomach when I collect the post each morning. It is ridiculous to say because he doesn't know I'm here. Or he has given up on me. But I don't believe that. In fact I imagine that the letters are still coming to the old house, but that because I didn't leave a forwarding address, they are growing mouldy in a drawer. Perhaps they are being thrown away. But yes, I feel certain that he hasn't given up. What can he possibly want from me? I imagine he is begging me to return to him, that he believes in some way that I belong there. I hate to see his writing sprawling across the grubby envelopes. I dutifully put each one in a box and tied it to the first as if I was building a raft. One day I will open them, one day when he is dead, and sail out to sea on them. But for now I am happy to stay on this grey island, where Seb sleeps so fitfully beside me as if he is guarding me from something and unable to fully commit to the act of sleeping. When we first met he could barely function. It took us so long to get to know each other. Every shared moment was the release of a held breath. If you truly love someone then everything you do together moves outwards to touch the walls of the house. I make the bed and I feel each thread between my fingers. I do not carry grief with me any longer. I'm not strong enough. My arms are too full.

In the hospital the sheets are folded so stiffly over Georgs's sleeping body that he looks like a table that has been set for lunch. A nurse is checking his drip and she nods at me curtly. I attempt to place his belongings in a sack by the foot of the bed and leave, but he wakes up and cries out to me.

'What is it, Georgs?' I ask.

'Please,' he says, his fingers creeping over the edge of the sheet and pinching at it desperately. 'My dog.'

He grabs at the nurse's leg and she turns her skinny neck to admonish him. They talk and she tells me, 'Mister Liepa would like you to take care of his dog.' She writes down an address in neat handwriting and gives it to me.

★

The stairwell of the hospital is rank with bleach and closed windows and sick breath. LEAVE NO FLOWERS IN THIS WARD is inked in square blue English capitals on a laminated sign. A door opens and a smell of meat wafts out, meat that has been cooked for too long, left out for too long, filling the rooms on taupe plastic trays above the chests of motionless people. Grey strings of the stuff. Hospitals, like airports, are the same all over the world. I am both comforted and repulsed by the sameness. I once watched my mother try and spoon something, a stew, into her own mother's mouth. 'I haven't any strength left,' the old woman said, 'and if I had the strength I wouldn't put that in my mouth and chew it, it smells all wrong to me.'

The address is an animal shelter just outside the city. A man with fists the size of Bibles leads me to where Georgs's dog lies with his nose jammed into the corner of his cage. He raises his yellow eye towards me and whines.

'You need to sign and then you can take,' the man says.

'Christ almighty,' I say, looking into the animal's face. He wags his tail weakly, but I can tell that he remembers who I am and that he is holding a grudge. In the corner of the cage is a barely chewed calf's foot. The guy in charge yawns and scratches his stomach as he holds the form and shows me where to sign. I don't know Georgs's address so I put Agnes's down instead.

'Come on, then,' I say to the dog. Outside he relieves his bladder in a fierce stream, squatting like a girl. The man, who has followed us to smoke a cigarette, leans against the door frame and laughs.

'You know why that happens,' he says. 'They remove the balls too soon. Very sad. Makes for very sad dog. You should have waited to remove the balls.'

'I didn't remove the balls,' I protest. The man just shakes his head and I lead the sad dog to the car, where Ursula is waiting for me. She sits with the engine running, tapping her hands on the wheel and singing loudly to the radio. She turns to see me shoving at the dog's backside and grins.

We drive to Riga. We hole up in a hotel room, a grungy place where a girl at reception shrugs meaninglessly when I ask about their policy regarding pets. I sit in the lobby, eating a Snickers bar and watching a flickering television. Ursula comes down, wearing her hair parted in the middle and tied back. It makes her look very serious. She also does not have a social smile; she only smiles when she is amused, and this makes her look serious too. In reality I think that there is a mischievous humour to everything that she does, although I'm not sure if it is truly her intention or only my interpretation of her idiosyncrasies. For instance, she can be so stern that I have no alternative but to laugh.

'How are you feeling?' I ask.

'I'm kind of up and down because of all the sugar I've been eating. I'm all over the place emotionally. I have to eat brown toast and eggs for the next twenty-four hours because I can't keep this up, honestly. Look at my hands.'

Her hands are trembling. I sidestep the obvious questions and decide to hold them between mine as a gesture of defiance. Or of masculinity. She twists them like a child trying to escape the grip of its father in order to run into traffic, a feeling I identify with.

'Oh. Stop. What are you doing?'

'Can I at least kiss you?'

'Just don't make a thing about it.'

The girl behind reception watches us kiss. We walk for a little while but Ursula is slow and distracted. She says it is because she is hyperglycaemic. Georgs's yellow-eyed dog walks behind us. The front of my trousers is completely grey with his hair, since the car ride frightened him and he lay with his enormous head and paws buried in my crotch, quivering as if I were taking him to be shot.

We find a cafe and Ursula expresses a desire to sit outside, although the sky is a steel grey and there is a faint mist of rain every so often. There are heaters on the terrace and the waitress, who is the happiest person I have so far seen in Latvia, brings over two red blankets that we spread over our laps. She notices the dog and spends a few minutes playing with him. For some reason he is still quivering. The waitress admonishes me. 'He isn't used to the city!' I tell her in protest. Eventually I end up wrapping my blanket around his torso like a cape. The waitress seems satisfied but Ursula looks at me from under a raised eyebrow. I explain that swaddling is very effective for canine anxiety. She says when her daughter was small and prone to tantrums she used to do the same thing. She mimics holding a small person so tightly that their arms are pinned to their sides, and laughs.

'You never mentioned that you had a daughter,' I say. Ursula shrugs.

'I'm a better mother in theory than in practice.'

'Okay,' I say, as if I know what she means. She tucks her blanket in around her legs so that she too is cocooned very tightly, and then she lights a cigarette. After a while she seems to forget that she lit it. She dangles her hand over the edge of the wooden seat and lets the wind burn it down to its filter, which she then carelessly lets fall from her fingers. A man who was previously playing the accordion comes to pick it up and put it in an ashtray. All of this happens as if they are players employed by the same circus, and I am a spectator.

I think about the first night I spent with Leda so many times that it feels now like a play that is constantly in motion, every movement rehearsed a thousand times, and every moment that follows already waiting in the wings. We spent so long together, the kissing growing tired, my tongue lapping at hers and then growing still in my mouth. I felt myself falling asleep. Eventually the clambering and rough housing seemed to grow pointless and I stopped. My lack of an erection seemed appropriate. She made me feel impotent as I had never felt before. She was so distant from me, so far away. Undressed, she slipped sheetways and slender to observe me from one propped arm and I winced.

'Oh, poor Seb.'

'I'm all right.'

'Oh, my poor Seb. Poor, poor.'

'I'm all right, I'm all right.'

'Oh.' She held my hand. She pitied me.

I remembered the stairs to the gallery again, the last space that I inhabited before knowing her. How far away those stairs, what a steep climb, the gallery smell, oh that deep clean carpet smell, or really an awareness that it was underfoot.

'I'm all right, I feel all right, let me look at you.'
I didn't want her to pity me.

I awoke. The things in the room seemed to murmur
to me. Leda slept facing away. I stared at the back
of her head and felt sick. The heat was unpleasant.
I slowly removed myself from the bed and stood
for a moment silently surveying the unfamiliar bed
where I had failed to fuck the most beautiful girl
I had ever seen, a phrase I would never speak out
loud, but still, I had failed to fuck her, and I achingly
slowly pulled my clothes back onto my body and
wore them out of the house and onto the street and
back slowly, through lone dog walkers and night
workers and taxis, slowly, slowly, back, home, alone,
a glass of water, a bald patch of carpet, my hot hands
on my face, unwashed, a window that would never
close properly and that let things in: moths, noises,
smells. A window that she would one day think of
as her own, and ask me to fix.

'The window.'

'Tomorrow.'

'*Mañana. Mañana. Mañana.*'

'I have faith.'

February 2005.

From the age of eight to fifteen I was put under the neglect-
ful care of my uncle and aunt in place of the (purpose-

fully?) distracted care of my single mother, Petra. It was a week after my father had died and I was sent to live with Uncle, Aunt, Olaf and Alex for a week while my mother recovered. It took ten days for her to decide that I should spend every weekend there, that their family was big enough to swallow me whole. By the end of that week I was spending my nights in Olaf's bed. There was nowhere else to put me. I spent the first few nights on a mattress at the end of my aunt and uncle's bed. But the weather changed and the baby Alex started crying in a high-pitched scream, his face all red, and wouldn't stop. There was a storm brewing and the air was close to our skin, breathing against our cheeks and making our lips swell, a diamond of perspiration in the philtrum. Olaf's bedroom was downstairs. You'll sleep better, my aunt said, kindly, her eyes bloodshot from sleep and Alex's little hand like a starfish opening and closing over her breast. Two yellow stains went from her nipples to her armpits and I swore to myself I'd never be a mother. The days were as reluctant to ebb as honey from a spoon.

Olaf and I slept under a single sheet and still it felt as if we were being pinned down by a wardrobe full of fur. I remember it when the sun shines relentlessly through the day and insists its heat upon the night. I sleep with my legs apart because I can't stand the feeling of my thighs sticking together. I throw my arms up and bury my face in the smell of the sweat that hides under them, my lungs full of myself.

Here's the thing: I was sleepless for three nights. I had gone semi-mad. The wind picked up around midnight and started throwing things at the windows. I turned as if to reach for the lamp and instead I got a fistful of his fingers. He held my hands either side of my face. I didn't know whether or not I was hallucinating, but I was so grateful that the window was open, and that flecks of warm rain began to hit my forehead, that I laughed.